$11.95

DEC 1983

S0-BBF-094

A Hanging at Tyburn

GILBERT B. CROSS

A Hanging at Tyburn

ATHENEUM · NEW YORK

· 1 9 8 3

Property of ... library stamp

LIBRARY OF CONGRESS CATALOGING IN PUBLICATION DATA

Cross, Gilbert B.
A hanging at Tyburn.

SUMMARY: A fourteen-year-old orphan with
a mysterious past is sentenced to death during
the turmoil of building the first cross-country canal
in eighteenth-century England.
[1. Canals—England—Fiction.   2. England—
Fiction.   3. Orphans—Fiction]   I. Title.
PZ7.C88252Han   1983   [Fic]   83-6331
ISBN 0-689-31007-2

Copyright © 1983 by Gilbert B. Cross
All rights reserved
Published simultaneously in Canada by
McClelland & Stewart, Ltd.
Composition by American Stratford Graphic Services, Inc.
Brattleboro, Vermont
Printed and bound by
Fairfield Graphics, Fairfield, Pennsylvania
Designed by Mary Ahern
First Edition

For my own "Triumvirate"
PEGGY · JOHN · ROBERT

Acknowledgments

There are many individuals and institutions to whom I am indebted. I received great assistance from the Walkden Public Library and the National Coal Board. Four people were particularly helpful. My cousin, Paul St. Pierre, spent several days with me tracing the course of the Duke's Canal. Elsie Mullineux's books on eighteenth century life and customs were invaluable, as was Hugh Malet's wonderful book, The Canal Duke. *Finally, I wish to thank Frank Mullineux, the acknowledged expert on the history of Worsley and the Bridgewater family. While this is not the book he claims to be "too lazy to write," I hope he will appreciate my version of the facts. To all those who contributed to this very pleasant ten year labor, especially my ever-patient family, my warmest thanks and appreciation.*

CONTENTS

I The Duke's Canal

II A Hanging at Tyburn

III A Castle in the Air

From underground emerging to the clouds;
Vessels o'er vessels, water under water,
Bridgewater triumphs—art has conquered nature

James Ogden, *"A Description of Manchester"* (1783)

1 Mercy and Irwell Navigation
2 Weaver Navigation
3 Thames River
4 Severn River
5 Trent River
6 Humber River
7 Clyde River

Glasgow

Edinburgh

Leeds

Manchester

Liverpool

Duke of
Bridgewater's
Canal

Stoke

Birmingham

Oxford

Cardiff

London

Bristol

THE WATERWAYS IN 1760

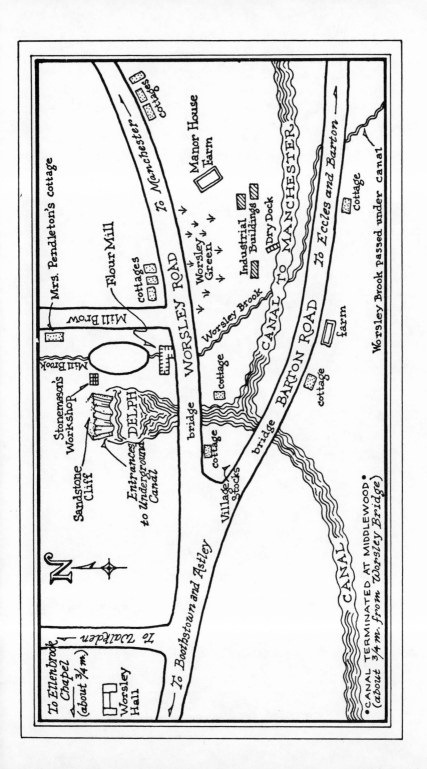

I

The Duke's Canal

N I G H T M A R E

"Do you forgive me?" asked the hangman.

"I do," I replied, "and may God have mercy upon our souls."

"Amen to that," he replied.

I should not live to see my sixteenth birthday. There was a slight tug on the rope to test it. The prison ordinary began chanting a psalm behind me.

"Ready?" asked the hangman.

"Aye," I said, kicking off my shoes.

From the crowd came a great roar of approval. Then silence. There was a violent crash, the trap dropped away beneath me, and I fell into the void.

*　*　*

C H A P T E R · 1

The German Giant

The year 1759 promised little more than the past one. It was cold and, far worse for a group of strolling players, the wettest February and March for years. I had just turned fourteen (as near as any of us could tell) and the leader of our troupe, Mr. Alfred L. Winstone, declared I should take a benefit performance.

" 'Tis only fair lad," he proclaimed to the pitiful few who made up The Sons and Daughters of Thespis, "for how else can a player eke out his meager stipend?"

He always talked that way. As for the benefit, I refused. I could scarcely ask the members of the company, each of whom was penniless, to perform free of charge on my behalf. And so it was that my fourteenth birthday passed without a single handbill announcing, "For the benefit of Mr. George Found."

The rest of the company were no doubt relieved at my sacrifice—though none of them said so.

"Well, I'll not force it upon ye, lad," said Mr. Winstone, "for in truth 'tis always a gamble. I knew one actor whose proudest boast was that he never *lost* more than five guineas at his ben."

It was in the nature of Mr. Winstone to remain cheerful whatever blows fate dealt us. True, his tricorne hat had lost some of its shape and the plumes had wilted, but he tried to maintain a certain elegance in his great wig, powder-blue overcoat and black leather shoes with silver buckles.

His wife, fat and ill-tempered, had enough pessimism for all. She complained from dawn to dusk, reminding all who would listen of the great sacrifices she had made in quitting Drury Lane to marry a strolling player. She was extraordinarily protective of her daughter, Cecilia, who resembled her in all things. Though the girl was almost fourteen, we still billed her as the "Infant Prodigy." And a ridiculous sight she was, too, playing little girls in a caraco jacket and cap of the French style.

The rest of the company was hardly worth the describing. An excessively thin fellow who went by the unlikely name of Horatio Prid and dressed always in a black preacher's gown had joined us in Birmingham. He generally played the leading young man parts though he was not good enough to be a utility. Miss Clarabella Snook, who simpered all the time and affected a lisp, was cast for heroines despite the fact that she could neither sing nor dance nor act. There were two more utilities, one called Kitterly, who forgot his lines, complained of a leg wound received in the '45, and reminded everyone that he had once met Colley Cibber. The other fellow spoke no language I ever heard, usually consoled himself with a large pot of porter, and played all nonspeaking roles.

Mr. Winstone was father to me, but he was not my natural father. I had no knowledge of my real parents. It was thought my mother died giving birth to me. Reared in a foundling home, I was given the name George in memory of the king. The surname "Found" was given me because as Mr. Pugg, the director of St. Dunstan's Home never tired of saying, "he was found and is a foundling."

I had run away from St. Dunstan's three years before because I was to be apprenticed to a catgut spinner. By begging, I kept myself alive, but after six months of freedom a fever seized me, and I collapsed in a delirium. I remembered nothing until I found myself staring up into the rubicund face of Mr. Alfred Winstone.

"Ah look, he moves, my sweet. A providential sign. I see in him a possible Romeo, Macbeth, finally a Richard to rival my own," he murmured.

My eyes beheld a strange sight. Bending over me was a portly man dressed in tight pantaloons, a large brown cloak, and a great buckled brown wig. He was gently wiping my forehead with a white lace handkerchief.

"I see in him another mouth to feed," was the sour response from a fat lady, who I later learned was Mrs. Winstone.

The manager rose to his feet still gazing down at me. "Ah then, my turtle dove, what if we bring him out in the starved business—the apothecary in *Romeo*, perhaps even as Sir Andrew Aguecheek?"

His good lady, his turtle dove, replied with a loud sniff, but Mr. Winstone beamed down at me.

And so I stayed. I did quite well in fact. We toured from small town to village. A large, slow-moving cart pulled by a weary horse carried our props and the females of the company while the men trudged alongside. But, for the first time in my life, I was happy. Mr. Winstone taught me to read and act. We made a little money and though we didn't eat well, we didn't starve. At St. Dunstan's the daily meal never varied—milk pottage for breakfast, pease soup for dinner. Mr. Winstone, with many quotes from drama and the Bible, easily justified poaching the odd rabbit or pheasant to liven up our evening meals on the road.

To speak honestly, his methods left much to be desired. He put out a handbill promising the most astounding novelties, never before seen, nay, dreamed of, in the town we were in. Then came the apology—sudden death, a shipwreck, a piece of treachery on the part of some ungrateful player who had absconded with his fee. As the audience began to register disapproval, he simply raised his hands and assured them that the few players who had remained faithful to him would perform Shakespeare's *Hamlet—without any cuts whatsoever*. This promise he never kept, for Mr. Winstone was always happy to get through a role without troubling himself to follow the exact words of the author. Indeed, he sometimes died at the wrong time and had to rise from the grave to finish the piece.

We were approaching Manchester by the way of Leigh Road when Mr. Winstone called a halt and summoned a council of war.

"As you know," he began, "this is not the best of times, but hope—"

"When do we get paid?" demanded Horatio Prid.

"Ahem," said the manager, trying to ignore him.

"Well?"

"I'm coming to that," replied Mr. Winstone. "We are not the first who with best meaning have incurred the worst. But, in short," he added hurriedly, "I have decided to stake all upon an appearance of the German Giant!"

There was complete silence. Finally the juvenile lead said hesitantly, "German giant?"

"Exactly."

"But we don't have any giant, German or otherwise," said Miss Snook with a sniff.

"That is where you are wrong," retorted Mr. Winstone drawing himself up magnificently, but somewhat spoiling the effect as his wig slipped over his left ear. *"I* am the German Giant."

"Ridiculous!"

"George, dear boy, please explain to those new to the company about the German Giant."

I stood before them. "It's a trick," I explained. "You may have seen the iron ball we keep in the bottom of the cart. Mr. Winstone can just lift it, but only because it is hollow. There is a bolt in it. Before the performance it will be filled with water and the bolt tightened. Then we call for two men to lift it onto the stage."

"Well, what's the point? He won't be able to lift it," replied her ladyship.

"When the ball is on the stage, the giant rolls it about until the bolt is over a small hole in the wood. I can then undo the bolt, let out the water, and Mr. Winstone can lift it."

"It's a silly idea," snapped Miss Snook.

"It is theater," stated Mr. Winstone magnificently.

"It's payday," said Horatio Prid, and that settled it.

Mr. Winstone dug among his effects and produced a dozen handbills.

"Show these around, George," he said, "and spread the word. Tell the local peasantry the German Giant will perform prodigiously on Astley Common tomorrow night at seven sharp. Seven sharp, mind."

The handbill proclaimed in dark black letters:

> SENSATIONAL ATTRACTION
> !! THE BAVARIAN GIANT !!
> !!! DIE DEUTSCHE COLOSSUS !!!
> !!!! WHO WILL LIFT TO HIS KNEES
> AN IRON BALL WEIGHING
> ALMOST ONE
> TON !!!!

There was quite a crowd. We had made a special effort to decorate the cart, which served as a backcloth to the half dozen wooden planks we called our stage. Ribbons hung from the trees, and though there was still some light left, several burning rush dips had been lit for the occasion.

We started with the wooing scene from Shakespeare's *Richard III*. The Infant Prodigy, for once, remembered Lady Anne's words, and Mr. Winstone was at his best.

After Richard came the celebrated dog Neptune, "engaged at prohibitive expense." Neptune sprang into a tank of water to rescue the Infant Prodigy from a watery grave. Of course, we had no dog, celebrated or otherwise. Mrs. Winstone wouldn't permit it. What we did was to find a stray dog (there were always plenty of them) and give it a few scraps for jumping into a small wooden tank of water.

When Cecilia "fell" into the tank (which when brimfull came scarcely up to her knees), the dog, hoping for more scraps, leaped in after her. They both scrambled out to very scattered applause.

The crowd was less than enthusiastic as I moved among them with my hat. A few coppers were thrown in, but most of the rougher sort thought it more sport to tweak my black wig bag as I passed. Those who did contribute were impatient to see the giant and hoped by their generosity to move things along. To tell the truth I was more than a little nervous. Lancashire and Cheshire audiences were far rougher than most and not likely to forgive any deception on our part.

I slipped away through the crowd, circling back behind them, and crawled under the stage, which was scarcely three inches above my head. Through peepholes in the wooden board I could see well enough.

There was a shout as Mr. Winstone walked quickly from behind the wagon dressed in a leopard skin and adorned with a huge, bushy false beard that effectively concealed most of his face. He stalked about the stage, glaring at the audience, which had now fallen silent, muttering loudly to himself in the most convincing German. Finally he eyed the iron ball lying beside the stage and stepped from the stage and seized a skinny man by the arm and led him to it. Motioning to him to lift the iron ball on to the stage, he retired to one side, folded his arms and gazed contemptuously at his victim. The poor fellow scratched his head, spat on his hands, rubbed them on his smock and bent to the task. He could just move it. A friend was summoned, a brawny fellow with only one tooth in his head. Together they raised it less than an inch, then it fell trapping the tip of the toothless one's fingers. The howls were genuine and convincing. The defeated pair returned to the crowd, one of them sucking on his fingers. His wife said loudly, "April noddy."

It took three men to position the iron ball on the stage and a great fuss they made, too. They should have; each was receiving a penny for his performance. The giant then placed his foot upon the ball and rolled it as if getting the feel of it. The stage creaked considerably even though the timbers had been specially strengthened that afternoon.

At last, as if seeming to tire of the sport, the giant rolled the ball center stage so the bolt was directly above me in the hole.

In my hand was a specially shaped piece of iron that fitted into the head of the bolt. With a few sharp twists the bolt would come off, there would be a deluge of water (carefully concealed beneath a drum roll played by the Infant Prodigy), and then I would replace the bolt, leaving the rest to the German Colossus.

But the bolt would not turn. Try as I might, it would not shift. Mr. Winstone soon sensed that something was amiss. He paused in his labors and stalked the stage as if to focus his strength. A few angry murmurs were heard above the drum rolls.

"Try lad, try," he muttered bending over the ball, back to the audience. "The thread must be crossed."

I tried my best but the bolt would not budge. Mr. Winstone, game to the last, almost pulled it off. With a superhuman effort, knowing all depended on him, he raised the ball six inches from the stage.

No one in the audience failed to hear the great sucking in of breath. Another inch. What could be seen of the giant's face was almost purple. He was directly above the hole where I lay. The lips moved in prayer. Another inch. There was a gasp and a ripple of applause as the iron ball moved another half inch towards knee height. Blood vessels pulsed in the giant's forehead, but the ball sank slowly to the stage.

We might have got away with it; I like to think that

Mr. Alfred Lewis Winstone would have carried the day. And so he might, had not the fellow whose fingers had been crushed taken his revenge. Shamed in front of his wife and neighbors, he seized the chance.

"Tha's nay German giant. And this is naught but a gypo," he shouted. "We'll teach thee a lesson, by God."

Mrs. Winstone, sensing that doom was near, rushed on stage. I'll say this for her, Rebecca Winstone proved herself a trouper to the last. "He is a German giant," she screamed; "I have the letters to prove it."

"Letters?" demanded five or six voices above the hubbub. "Show us the letters."

She reached into her ample bosom and produced several of the letters her husband had written before they were wed.

"Here," she said, waving them before the mob. "Who amongst ye can read High German?"

That did it, of course. Mr. Winstone tore off his false beard and went down on one knee before them, but two ruffians black with coal dust tossed him to one side, big though he was.

I rolled out from under the stage unnoticed in the melée. We all took to our heels, but no one was after us. I saw four men roll the iron ball into a ditch. The rest contented themselves with rocking our wagon until it fell on its side, breaking one of the wide iron-banded wheels. Boots, wigs, hats, feathers, canes, and cloaks tumbled out and were trodden underfoot. Several burly children ripped down the tattered banner that announced the German Giant's appearance.

We gathered at a safe distance from the uproar. Mr. Winstone sat on a tree stump, surveying the damage; the Infant Prodigy was weeping, and her mama had a handkerchief to her eyes. I felt like crying myself. Of the rest of our company, there was no sign.

"Well, George," said the manager with a sigh, looking strangely out of place in a leopard skin, *"that* was something like a farewell performance."

At this Cecilia broke into loud sobs; I felt hot tears run down my cheeks.

"Nay, lad, fall not thy tears," he said, putting his arm around my shoulders, "I hope well of tomorrow. No more onion-eyes. Let's to supper and drown consideration."

But the Infant Prodigy just sobbed all the louder.

CHAPTER · 2

Worsley Delph

We spent a miserable night. No sooner was it safe for us to return to the wreckage of the wagon than it began to rain.

Mr. Winstone was up before all of us. I heard him rummaging through the ruins.

"Ah, George," he said. " 'Tis almost time for the rosy fingered dawn to make an appearance, but I fear 'twill be no sight to gladden the eye."

And indeed it wasn't. I found my tricorne hat and my Sunday best dark frock coat in a hamper. It scarcely matched my green breeches, but that was of little concern. Mrs. Winstone and the Infant Prodigy would have continued their wailing of the night before, but the manager set them to work lighting a fire and sorting what was left of our props.

The cart lay on its side like a gaudy whale. One wheel was broken and several boards had sprung loose.

"We'll never right her, lad," said Mr. Winstone, "for

she weighs more than that damned iron ball."

"She lies on a slight incline," I pointed out. "If we can cut a stout enough branch from one of these trees, we might be able to lever it upright."

"A Daniel came to judgment," breathed the manager. "Let us see if those bumpkins have left either of the swords."

We found one. The tip had been broken off, but there was enough blade to hack off a stout ash branch. We slid the limb under the floor of the wagon and both of us lifted. With a crash, the cart fell back on its three good wheels.

By noon the world looked fairer. The rain stopped and a watery sun made an appearance. Manuscripts and wigs (our most expensive items) were carefully laid out to dry on a large rock.

Mr. Winstone surveyed them.

"Fashion's a strange whim, George," he said. "Look what we wear—full flowing wigs, hats that don't cover 'em, three cornered ones at that. And what the devil does a man do with long waistcoats, shoes with silver buckles, lace neckcloths, white ruffles, and silk stockings?"

" 'Tis strange, sir."

"Now a wig," he continued, ignoring me, "is a great leveller, its curls stop the ravages of time; a bald head is a tiresome thing, but a wig is no laughing matter, either. It must be dressed and curled and, worst of all, powdered. George, I remember when I was in the cavalry. We seldom charged I'll admit, but when we did, half the wigs fell off before the first volley. And I have often noted the better classes seldom exercise for fear their wigs should fall."

He stayed in this reverie for some time, then reached into his pocket and let out a roar of anger.

"My watch," he exclaimed, " 'tis gone. I left it in the charge of that fustian rascal, Prid, when I changed into the leopard skin. 'Tis halfway to Manchester by now, I'll warrant. The burghers of Calais presented me with it after I appeared in *Richard III*." He turned from me, a tear in his eye. "Well, God made him, and therefore, let him pass for a man."

"I don't suppose we will see the rest of The Sons and Daughters of Thespis again," I said after he had regained his composure.

"Nay, lad, that we won't. When a manager fails, the actors generally abandon him as rats swim for their lives when a ship founders. They're gone, and good riddance, say I."

We held an accounting over a midmorning meal of bread and overripe cheese. My share was the pennies I had collected in the hat before the end of the German Giant. The grand total was ninepence three farthings. Mrs. Winstone took a guinea from her great bosom and stuffed a couple of muddy letters back in its place. The Infant Prodigy found a coin that bent between her father's teeth.

"Counterfeit," he commented "still 'twill serve."

Our cashbox had been forced, but that was nothing new. Over the years several highwaymen had demanded it in exchange for our lives. We always gave it willingly, for it never held anything more than the odd few pence. Any real money was kept under a board in the wagon. From this hoard, Mr. Winstone produced three gold guineas.

"Not much for a life devoted to the Muse," said the manager, "but we have our health. The family, though small, is safe, and three guineas will set me up in a new line of work."

"New line of work?" His lady snorted. "What new line of work? You were always an actor."

Mr. Winstone drew himself up, adjusted his wig, clapped on his hat, and struck a pose of injured dignity. "I was in the cavalry, my sweet."

"For three years."

He ignored her and continued in the same determined tone. "And do you suppose that a man of my caliber can do nought else but act?" he demanded. "I shall do what other gentlemen have done when battered by the blows of fate. I shall ride the high toby, become, in short, a highwayman!"

Mrs. Winstone let out a scream and clapped her hands to her mouth; the Infant Prodigy burst into tears, but the manager remained unmoved.

"But why?" I asked in amazement. "Surely there must be something else?"

"My dear George. Gentlemen of the road are mainly of my class. They are the aristocracy of crime, very particular who joins their ranks. They'll have no truck with ruined farmers and cast-off servants. Amongst them I shall be respected and accepted. The cart must be sold; probably to the nearest wheelwright. That income and these gold coins will provide for a brace of pistols and a spavined nag. Within a year I shall be restored to wealth and position."

At this both women dissolved into fresh tears.

"Come, come, no tears," he ordered, "for destiny will have it so. I shall rob the rich and give to the poor, in short, myself.

"George," he said, turning to me. "Here's a guinea. Nay," he added, as I began to protest. "I wish it could be more. You were the son I never could have and a guinea is a poor patrimony. Now come to my arms."

We embraced. And then, miraculously, I was in the arms of his lady and then the Infant Prodigy. There was a salty taste in my mouth.

"Head for Manchester, George, that's my advice. 'Tis less than two or three days easy walking. The town is growing apace, and a lad of your mettle will certainly find something."

We parted very soon after. I headed east along the Leigh Road. I looked back only once; they were all sitting on the wagon; Mr. Winstone gave a wave of his handkerchief.

The first miles passed quickly enough. Once beyond the village I found myself walking by fields and occasional cottages. Most fields were plowed and waiting for the spring planting. From time to time I saw women and children picking stones from new-plowed fields to be used on the turnpike roads. By a stream several children were

Property of Rochambeau
Middle School Library

picking rushes. These they told me would be dipped in tallow to make candles for use in a nearby coal pit.

It began to get dark, and I was anxious to find a place to spend the night. Luck was with me, for round the next bend in the road stood a tumbledown barn. Creeping inside I discovered there was just enough light to see a huge brown rat calmly foraging for food among a pile of turnips. So hungry was I that I bit into a turnip myself. The rat, never really frightened, twitched his whiskers, flicked his tail, and leaped from turnip to turnip into the safety of a dark hole. In the darkness I could see the angry fire-red eyes glaring at me.

I made a bed for myself on a pile of clover and hay using a giant plaited straw basket as a pillow.

Sleep did not come easily that night. Exhaustion, fear for Mr. Winstone's life, and my uncertain future, pressed heavily upon me. I tossed many hours before a fitful slumber came over me, but not for long.

I awoke with a cry of terror; sweat pouring down my face. I had had the dream again—the fearful nightmare that haunted me. I was in a wooden cart, my elbows pinioned to my side. A man with a black bandage on his eyes was riding alongside. On all sides was a vast multitude of people who seemed to be shouting, yet no words could I hear. Ahead, and slowly rising from the earth as the cart laboriously climbed a low hill, was a huge wooden gallows.

In terror I snatched up my hat and frock coat and fled into the early morning mist. I had nothing to eat for a day; pangs of hunger were gnawing inside me. A damp, fine misty drizzle shrouded everything from view; trees loomed out of the mist like specters.

I stumbled on, falling more than once. In the distance there was the bark of a fox and, nearer, the sound of a door slamming. Each step exhausted me as the wet clay dragged me down. Finally I reached a wooded slope, grateful to escape the teacherous ooze. There I scraped the clay from my shoes with a hazel stick. The smell of leaf mold was dank; everywhere there was the sound of water dripping from leaf to leaf and from leaf to ground.

The land rose before me; trees gave way to dense bushes. I could hear the sound of water nearby. I forced my legs to climb the steep hill; there was a sharp pain in my chest, but at last the ground began to level off. When the mist cleared, I would have a commanding view of the countryside for miles around.

With this new hope, I took a final step. Abruptly the earth gave way beneath me. I plunged through space and then, with a blow that knocked every scrap of breath from my body, fell into the foulest tasting water in the length and breadth of all England.

CHAPTER · 3

Icarus

I rose to the surface kicking and spluttering. The icy water was but a few feet deep, and I had hit the bottom with such violence that every bone in my body felt as if it were broken.

A voice from far away cried out, "Hold on there, lad," and a strong arm dragged me from the icy water onto rocky ground.

I tried to speak out but could not. My head was ringing, and the water in my lungs made me fight for breath. Two men lifted me onto a sheep hurdle and carried me into a nearby mill. Then they placed me on a pile of flour sacks and stripped off my wet clothes. One of them placed a wool blanket over me.

With an effort I opened my eyes. Dazzling lights danced before me, but as they cleared I was able to see about me. A candle burned on a nearby shelf and three men, two of whom were gentlemen, not laborers, were looking down on me.

The taller one spoke. "I've sent Mrs. Pendleton for brandy, your grace."

At that moment, a woman of about forty appeared, bearing a glass. She was sparrowlike and her face was kindly. "He's awake, your grace?"

"Barely, Mrs. Pendleton, barely. I doubt if he can understand ought. Have ye seen him before?"

"No, your grace, he's not from Worsley. Nor has he the look of a weaver or a miner's lad."

The man addressed as "your grace" helped raise me up, and the woman tilted the glass to my lips. A fiery liquid coursed down my throat. A fresh spasm of coughing followed. "Steady lad," said the second gentleman. "French brandy is hard to come by in these times."

"Did he cough any blood?" the woman asked him.

"None," he replied.

"Then we must move him to my house. Happen he'll do better there than in t'mill."

The sheep hurdle was fetched, and I was carried up a steep hill into a small stone cottage and placed on a bed in a narrow back room curtained off from the living quarters.

"Aye, this will suit," said his grace. "But ye'll not be the loser by it, Mrs. Pendleton. Can you board him at say fifteen . . . a shilling a week until we find out more about him?"

"Very generous, your grace," replied Mrs. Pendleton with the trace of a smile about her lips.

"Come then, John, there's work to be done, and the

day is slipping by. We must inspect the sough this very hour."

The two men left, and I slept fitfully. When I woke it was dark outside. A fire burned in the grate; the curtain had been taken down. A girl of about my age, dressed in a thick flannel dress and wearing a white cap, was eating at the table. She was bright-eyed but pale, there being little bloom to her cheeks. She looked up and spoke.

"Well, who is 'e, Ma?"

"How should I know, child. You can tell he's not from hereabouts."

The girl left the table and sat on the edge of the bed. "He's a bit skinny, ain't he? How old do you think he is, Ma?"

"Bless me child, he can't be no more than fifteen. I'd say he's bin on the road a while by the look of his clothes. He's a good-looking boy, isn't he. Look at the blue in his eyes."

The girl sniffed and tossed her head back. "Well, he's no miner, look at his fingernails."

"He had a nightmare too, lass. Though 'tis not surprising after a fall in t'Delph."

"What about, Ma?"

"Lord child, how do I know? He shouted about a man with black bandages over his eyes. And—" She broke off.

"Go on, Ma?"

"He talked about a scaffold."

"A scaffold?"

"Aye, child, a scaffold."

"You mean a hanging scaffold."

"Aye."

The daughter looked at me. "Can you hear me?"

"Yes."

"What's yer name?"

"George."

"George what?"

"George Found."

"Silly name," said the girl with a sniff. "Who ever 'eard of it?"

"Now, Peg," warned the mother, "you mind your manners. Listen to the way he talks, he's an educated lad. He doesn't speak like us."

"And what's wrong with the way I speaks, Ma?" demanded the girl indignantly.

"Nothing at all, lass, for Worsley, but tha can tell he's not working class."

"Well, I can see that, Ma," replied the girl, not the least won over. "Look at his hands, not a seg on 'em. 'E's the son of some clergyman or fat Liverpool merchant."

Her mother took a linen handkerchief, wetted it in a wooden basin and carefully wiped my forehead. "I don't think so, Peg dear; he sounds more like Lunnon folk to me."

"Oh Ma. When was you ever in London?"

"I went there twice, Miss Pert, if you must know, for the old Duke. And anyway, I said, *like* Lunnon folk. There are travelers come through Worsley."

"Well, what are we to do with 'im?"

"He's to stay here. In the back room, by his grace's order."

"But Ma," wailed the girl, "that's my room."

"Now child, it'll be but a short while afore he's no longer poorly."

"Well, let 'im stay at the Hall with 'is grace, if he's so precious."

"Now, Peg," said the mother, rising to her feet, "I'll not have you speak disrespectful of his grace. Thanks to him there's work hereabouts, and don't you forget it. He could have stayed in Lunnon gambling his money away, but no, he came back, and there's work in his mines for all who's sober and reliable."

"I don't know Ma," replied Peg, crossing the room and poking the fire, "there's water in the lower workings again. Johnny Aston and Brevis Owdhammer were going in to gin it out."

"The sough?"

"Aye, it silts up all the time, and the coal is much deeper up at Edge Fold in Crombouke and Brassey seams. Roger Entwistle told me they could float sleds out at Cuppin's Croft."

Both of them were silent for a long time, then the mother said briskly, "Well, let's try to get some broth into the lad. And tak' down the gingerbread mold, we'll see if some parkin will please him."

But during the next few days I got worse not better. Fever seized me. One moment I would be sweating, the next shivering. Blankets were sent down from the Hall and piled on me; the next minute I had thrown them off the bed. Trips to the outside privy were agonizing. Peg stayed home to help her mother, for someone had to sit with me night and day.

I heard snatches of conversation, anxious faces looked down on me. A doctor was summoned, then another. I was bled profusely. Once a day Doctor Cage came out and cut my veins. Blood poured into the cup Mrs. Pendleton held.

"He's to be blooded each day—nine or ten ounces," said Doctor Cage. "Give him a draught of dried liverwort and black pepper in goat's milk each morning."

Mrs. Pendleton tried the cordial only once. Weak though I was, I would not stomach it. A broth was ordered in its place. Dr. Cage would not hear of any change in bleeding me. Dark wormlike creatures called leeches were placed on my arms to suck the blood. When full, they dropped from me and were carefully kept for the next day's letting.

After three days I was worse. A Dr. Crippen from Barton was sent for.

"Leeches cost fourpence each," he muttered looking down at me through spectacles, "but they don't take out enough blood. You, ma'am, must use the knife. Also he's to have snail tea. I believe in it. Boil two or three snails in barley water and let him drink it late at night."

The following day Mrs. Pendleton was nervous as she attempted to bleed me. She cut too deep, and I lost so much blood that Dr. Cage had to be sent for immediately. He ordered brandy from the Grapes, the local inn, to restore me.

"Let him alone tomorrow," he advised.

The next day I felt stronger and took some broth. Peg looked thoughtful as she sat by the fire.

When her mother came to bleed me next, the daughter said, "Let 'im be Ma, the bleeding does 'im no good."

"But Peg, the doctor said . . ."

"Oh, the doctor," said the girl impatiently. " 'E says there's no hope. Give 'im some more broth. If 'e gets worse we can bleed 'im tomorrer."

"Well . . ." said her mother, doubtfully.

"Go on Ma, cook up some broth. I'll go down to Mr. Booth's for a loaf of fine white bread."

"White bread, Peg?"

"White bread, Ma."

The next day I was much better. The doctor saw me and pronounced me past the worst.

"Continue the bleeding," he ordered.

But instead I got fine white bread soaked in rabbit or chicken broth. My nights were better; I had no more nightmares.

Three weeks after I had been declared beyond hope, I was well enough to sit in front of the smoky fire and do light labor such as making rush dips to light the house. Mrs. Pendleton and I also made candles for Peg to use in the coal mine.

At six in the evening, Peg would come from the

mine with a thick canvas belt and iron chain slung over her shoulder. Black coal dust covered her from her wooden clogs to her cotton headscarf.

Although she had saved my life, she still regarded me with suspicion. I had surprised her one evening by reading from a copy of *Pilgrim's Progress* that lay on the window ledge.

"Well," she said with a sniff, "we are full of surprises."

Her mother just smiled.

One rainy evening, some three weeks after the worst of my illness had passed, the three of us were sitting by the fire as I read from *Pilgrim's Progress*. Outside we heard the sound of the Duke of Bridgewater's carriage stopping in front of the cottage. There was a great deal of excitement and fussing by Mrs. Pendleton before he was seated in the best chair before the fire.

"Well," he said surveying me carefully, "a miracle has certainly taken place. Lazarus has risen from the grave."

This was my first real opportunity to see the duke. I found him a young man, much younger than I expected. He looked scarce twenty; his face was quite unexceptional; occasional smallpox scars and eyebrows of different heights certainly did not make him handsome. And his clothes were far from elegant. The frock coat was brown with gold buttons and the frogs had pulled loose in several spots. The red collar was ripped on one side, and his waistcoat was stained with snuff.

"Can you stand lad?"

I rose and bowed from the waist.

"Nay, lad," he replied, motioning me back to my chair, "no ceremony here." He seemed pleased though.

"I am Francis, Third Duke of Bridgewater. 'Twas I and my agent, Mr. Gilbert, who flushed you from Worsley Delph."

"I am grateful, sir. I hope to recompense you if it should lie in my power."

His grace seemed a little taken aback. I heard him murmur. "A very pretty answer. This is no pit boy." I also heard a loud sniff from the far side of the table. Out of the corner of my eye, I saw Mrs. Pendleton deliver a smart nudge to her daughter's waist.

"He's been well schooled, your grace," said Mrs. Pendleton, "and was a strolling actor. Imagine! He reads like the parson."

"Better I hope," replied the duke drily. I had already heard that he had not paid his tithes in some months, preferring to spend the money on his coal mines.

"Well, read me a passage, if you will."

I chose the passage of Faithful's trial in the city of Vanity Fair, his spirited defense and speech to the jury. Even Peg seemed moved.

"Very fine," commented the duke, taking a large pinch of snuff, some of which spilled onto his waistcoat. There was a loud sneeze. Mrs. Pendleton tried hard not to smile. "Very fine indeed. I shall call you 'Icarus,' George. Do you know why, George?"

"The only Icarus I know, your grace, flew too near the sun and his waxen wings melted."

"Capital" said the duke, "and down he plunged into the sea. Just as you fell from a great height into my water."

He reached into his pocket and drew forth a large clay pipe and tin of tobacco. He took a rush from the floor and stuck it in the fire, using it as a taper.

"But sithee, Icarus," he said, drawing the flame into the bowl of his pipe, "there's precious little work around here for book readers. And strolling players are not much in demand."

"I will do any tasks, sir."

"Aye, aye, I know you will. I take you to be a likely lad that's not one to be beholden to others. Do you think you could help win coal? This is mining country, Icarus, or t'would be if the damn—begging your pardon, ma'am—if the sough would only drain the headings."

"But your grace," Peg burst out, "he knows nought of mines. He cannot tell the difference between cannel and turf."

"He can push a sled of coal, can he not?" demanded the duke.

"Well, sir, he is still weak," said Mrs. Pendleton.

"I know, I know, but he'll start slow and work up to the full twelve hours," decided the duke. "Peg will show him what to do. It's decided, Icarus," he added, puffing deeply on his pipe. Then he took it from his mouth and pointed the stem at me. "I'll set you on and see how you go. When you do a full day, you'll be paid at the rate of half a man."

At this there was a shout of dismay from Peg. Even the duke seemed a little shaken. "And," he continued hurriedly, "Peg will get an extra penny a day for her trouble."

Calm was eventually restored, but the duke didn't stay long. Peg retired to a corner for the rest of the evening, muttering darkly about being nursemaid to some great babby and threatening me with the fright of my sissy life when she got me a mile underground.

As for me, I knew I should give a good account of myself. After all, what could be difficult about digging coal?

Which just goes to show how wrong a person can be.

CHAPTER · 4

Darkness Visible

Three days later Doctor Cage declared me fit enough to work in the mine.

"Not a full day, mind," he ordered, "eight hours will be sufficient."

Long before dawn Worsley was astir, I could hear the knocker-up banging on the doors and windows of those of us who were to work the day shift.

I dressed hurriedly in a coarse flannel shirt and trousers that Mrs. Pendleton had found for me and drew back the curtain. The widow was bustling about preparing oatmeal in a large pan while her daughter was sloshing cold water on her face. She wore a thick dress of a dark brown flannel material.

"Morning, George," said Mrs. Pendleton; her daughter said nothing. "I've a special treat for you two—hot chocolate." We drank it gratefully, hands pressed against our mugs for warmth in the predawn chill.

"Tommy ready, Ma?"

"Always is, isn't it?" replied Mrs. Pendleton, placing two tin boxes on the table. This, I gathered, was our lunch.

"George, his grace sent you a pair of boots," she said, pointing to a stout pair of leather boots lying by the fireplace.

"Come on then," Peg snapped, as I struggled to get the boots on. "Pick up them candles and get that hat on."

We walked briskly down the lane to the mine entrance. The sun would not rise for another hour. Other miners were leaving their cottages. A dank mist muffled the sound of boots and clogs on cobblestones and gave miners slipping from their houses the appearance of wraiths. Some miners carried shovels with them, others short lengths of wood. One or two carried picks. I knew they were not hewers, for the men who actually cut the coal had entered the mine hours before. These picks were to replace those dulled by constant hacking and hewing at the duke's "black diamonds."

The boys and girls generally carried belts like Peg's. Everyone carried candles; some were already wedging them into spikes. A few called out a friendly greeting to us, but most kept their thoughts to themselves.

At the bottom of Mill Brow stood the mill and the mine entrance. The workers were already entering long narrow boats and disappearing through a double wooden door that covered the entrance. Yellow water poured out into the basin.

"T'basin," said Peg, as we drew close to an almost stagnant pool at the base of a sandstone cliff. "And over there's the mill," she muttered, "where they first brought you, and on the right is the sough."

I don't know what I had expected, though the yellowness of the water was striking. I looked up the sheer side of the sandstone quarry.

"You were lucky," she commented, "for 'tis over a hundred feet and sometimes there's little water in the basin."

The entrance to the mine was no more than a tunnel from which flowed a yellow stream.

"That's the sough," Peg said. "Takes water from headings. Trouble is seams get lower under Walkden Moor, and the water backs up because it don't take out enough. Some seams are so low that hewers 'ave to be brought out if it rains."

I suppressed a shudder. Under the ground we would be at the mercy of the weather we knew nothing of.

"Two hewers were all but drowned last week. Come on!"

She led the way to one of the leaky boats.

"What causes the color of the stream?" I asked.

"Water leaching from underground springs in the mine. Duke says it's sommat to do with salts of iron. 'E says it's healthy to drink. *Tha* know better. Now, get up front," she ordered.

I climbed into the wooden boat. At once a fine black dust filled my lungs, and I started sneezing.

"Tha'll get used to that," my guide said, "plenty more on the inside."

She took a thick ash pole from the floor of the boat. "From Worsley, this is the only entrance to the mine unless tha wants to wade in. Not many does 'cause they'll be in there for twelve hours happen, without they're hewers o'course. They can be done in eight."

The bow of the boat bumped against the doors.

"Hold 'em open and get yer 'ead down."

I did as ordered, and we slid into a narrow tunnel, the top of which was now but three feet from the top of the boat. Both of us had to keep our heads down as we scraped past the door and were plunged into instant blackness.

At once panic seized me. I wanted to cry out, to flee that foul place. For an instant I saw myself in my nightmare, falling through the trapdoor into the dark, gaping hole below.

And then, bringing me sharply back to reality, I heard Peg speaking, her words echoing from the cavern walls.

"Art tha deaf now?" she demanded in a familiar voice and tone. "I said, feel in front of yoursel' and pass me the flint and a candle."

I fumbled on the floor of the boat, my hands still shaking, found the flint and a fat mutton candle and felt for her hands; they were rough and hard to the touch. There were several sharp scrapes of flint against iron. Sparks flew and suddenly, a candle flamed.

"Stick this on the front of the boat with the droppings. If tha can't manage it, then hold it."

Already she had lit a second candle and using the mutton fat droppings as glue, she stuck it on the stern.

"The candles are brighter than wax," I commented.

"Well, we don't burn wax candles down a mine. Tallow's cheaper, and we add a little arsenic to them—makes 'em burn brighter."

She began poling us along. " 'Tis 'alf a mile before we get out," she said between grunts. "All the workings is drained by this sough. But won't be much longer. There's water in the deeper workings and the mines are all worked out above this level."

I was surprised at her strength. She was poling two of us and an eight-foot boat with ease. Since the roof was low she had to kneel in the bottom of the boat. I sneezed several more times, and each time there was a grim laugh from the stern.

Occasionally we pulled into the side as loaded boats went by. Everyone seemed to know Peg. Some lads of my age whistled at her, and she splashed water on one of them extinguishing his candle. She didn't seem to resent their attention though. I sensed she was embarrassed at having to accompany me.

At first, the darkness seemed to engulf me. It was as if a curtain lay before us, and I wanted to reach out and part it, but as we entered the tunnel, my eyes slowly became accustomed to the gloom, and I could see by the light of our candles that the tunnel was mainly carved from rock. Sometimes, there was a short section of brick.

The smell was of damp, as if a place long closed was being opened up.

Peg had no time for me. She continued to pole the boat, humming tunelessly. I forced myself to pay attention to the scene around us. Twice we passed underground wharves where groups of figures tipped coal from baskets into narrow boats. Candles fixed in the walls cast an eerie glow around. Men, and even some women, were stripped to the waist, glistening with black sweat.

Then we were gone, and silence surrounded us once more.

"All of atremble are yer?" asked Peg unexpectedly.

"Well I . . ."

"We all 'ad them. The trembles, I mean. Tha'll feel better once we get to work. Soon be there now."

My hands were no longer shaking, but it was a great relief when we reached the end of the sough and scrambled out onto the solid rock of a small basin. Some lads were tipping coal from baskets into boats tied up opposite the end of a dark tunnel. Two black shapes scurried from it and silently entered the water. I shuddered. Peg laughed.

"Rats mean it's safe. When they start runnin' you run too. Come on."

Peg was leading the way down a passage carved from solid rock. I hastened my pace. Something caught me a resounding blow on the head. I cried out, staggered, and fell to the ground; Peg came back. She wasn't very sympathetic.

"Tha's got ter look *up* as well as *down* in a mine," she

said, relighting my candle and clamping my hat back on. "Tha'll 'ave a bump there as big as a thrush's egg, but that's nothing new. Tha falls a lot, after all."

"I thought it would be an even six feet all the way."

"Tha daft fool. This is the main road, wait 'til tha sees the headings."

We moved more slowly now as the road began to slope sharply. A voice in the distance shouted, "Haud off!"

"Move yerself," ordered Peg as out of the darkness came a girl about her age. She was scarcely a foot from us as she passed. By the light of my candle, I could see her face plainly. Her eyes were bright. She winked at me, eyes sparkling under lashes thickly clogged with black dust.

"Mornin' Peg. Showin' im the ropes, is it?"

She disappeared with a short laugh. There was a broad canvas belt around her waist, and a chain ran from it between her legs to a wooden sled on iron runners. A second, smaller girl was pushing from behind. Both of them were breathing hard and glistening rivers of sweat made streaks of white through the coal dust on their faces.

"See that?" asked Peg.

"Yes."

"The fool at front is Ada Gregory; she's a drawer. T'other one is her sister, Nelly, she's a thrutcher. They pulls the sledges to the sough and then tips coal in the boats."

"Who digs our coal?"

"Coal is got or won, not dug, yer daft fool. We works for Black Tom and Joe. Tom ain't got kids. Joe'll be a hewer one day. Tom's best hewer around. He's never taken a pick handle to me which is more'n most can say."

A second sled went by, we hugged the wall.

"Each basket 'as two hundredweight coal in it," said Peg. "Ten on 'em makes a ton. We fills two score each shift."

"Forty baskets!"

"Tha'll need more than fancy talk down 'ere. Tha shapes up or else."

The ground rose gently before us. There was a sound of singing and of metal striking rock. Narrow tunnels led off from the main road; occasionally there was a glimmer of light at the end.

"Why are they singing?" I asked.

"Some sings, some swears, and some like Black Tom does neither. 'E's respected. Strongest man in t'mine."

She ducked into a narrow side tunnel no more than four feet high. I followed holding my candle in front of me. At one point we were forced to creep on hands and knees as the roof came to within three feet of the ground. Again fear seized me; I began to tremble. What we were doing must be wrong. Above us were millions of tons of rock waiting to crush us to pulp. God had never intended men to crawl in the bowels of earth like animals. I had an almost irresistible urge to stand upright, to straighten my back.

"Come on," she said, "the day's almost passed, and there'll be baskets awaiting."

The passage widened slightly, and we were in a room hewed out of solid coal. Two pillars of coal had been left to support the roof. At the far end, a huge man stripped to the waist was on his knees; his body was as black as the coal around us. Several lighted candles cast a faint glow in the area he had carefully hollowed out. In his hands was a pick, a heavy oak staff with a cross piece tipped at both ends with iron. He drove it into the coal, paused for an instant, then jerked on the pick handle. A huge lump of coal, followed by several smaller ones fell to the ground. A lad similarly dressed, and just as black, moved forward with a shovel and loaded the coal carefully into baskets. A great pile of baskets lay against one wall.

"Mornin' Tom, Joe."

"Morning, Peg, or is it gone noon?"

" 'Tis only gone six."

"That late, eh?" He grinned. "What's the weather?"

"Cold and misty."

"Funny, 'tis warm enough here," replied the miner, laughing at his own joke. "Who's that with thee?"

"Lad as fell into basin. Name's George."

"Oh, aye."

"Duke wants 'im to be a drawer. At 'alf a man," she added angrily.

"That's generous. Come forward lad, let's tak' a look at thee."

I moved forward in a crouch.

"So tha wants to be a miner?"

"Yes, sir."

Peg gave a short laugh.

Tom ignored her. "Tha can call me Tom, most do."

He was a giant of a man, whose nose had been broken. Stripped to the waist, he wore nothing on his feet. Elbows and knees were covered with thick leather patches, and his hair was tied back in a queue and fastened with, of all things, a neat blue bow. Muscles rippled across his chest. Even in the poor light, where there was no coal dust I could see thin blue scars tracing their way across his body.

"Well, George, tha can have Joe's job when tha's ready. He won't mind—time he became a hewer any 'ows." He sat on a lump or rock and picked up a pipe lying nearby.

"Does tha see them notched sticks over there, George?"

"Yes, Tom."

"We sticks one of them in each basket of coal to keep count. To make our wages, we must fill and carry out two score a day. Mostly we use what's called the pillar and stall method of getting coal. Them pillars of coal over there"—he pointed to them—"holds up the roof. Later, when we's bored with life, we starts getting coal from the far pillars, movin' slowly back to the main road."

"But what supports. . . ?"

He gave a hearty laugh. "The roof falls in behind us. 'Tis a great life, George. I wouldn't have it any other way.

I come in early and leave when ah've done mi lot." He groped along a ledge and produced a leather pouch of tobacco and began stuffing his pipe.

"Tom here is a putter. He puts the coal in the baskets, you and Peg load 'em on the sled and draws 'em down to the boats. Tha'll be a thrutcher for a trip or two. You push from behind ter get the feel on't. Both of yer kecks—that means tips—coal in t'boats at end of road. Nothin' to it really." He leaned to the side and used a flickering candle to light his pipe. *"If* tha can do it twelve hours a day, six days a week. If tha needs help, just sing out."

"Thank you, Tom."

" 'T'aint much of a life, and tha's not the look of a collier's son. I mean that kindly. This is not easy labor, even for them as knows now't else."

"He's to be a drawer, Tom" said Peg, "there's no thought of him getting coal."

The giant laughed. "We'll see. If he's a likely lad, why shouldn't he be a hewer? After we build him up o'course."

Peg turned to me. "Come on, then."

For the next two hours, Peg dragged and I thrust, my head against the baskets. That was bad enough, but there was worse, far worse, to come.

Peg took off her canvas belt and chain and handed it to me. "Tak' this belt and put it round tha waist. No. Not too tight or tha'll never catch tha breath. You'll have boils big as onions if it rubs. Now hook the chain to it.

This way," she said, impatiently. "Then get down on your hands and knees and put it between tha legs."

She dragged one of the sleds over. "The hook fits into the catband. So. Now pull it to the main road."

It wasn't easy. Twice the chain tangled up in my legs and cut deeply into my thigh. Even worse was the pain in my knees and the palms of my hands as I crawled along. Peg followed behind. At one point the hook came out of the catband and gave me a painful blow on the back.

"Half a man," I heard her mutter, "the duke's taken boggarts, he's mad."

When we reached the main road she shouted. "Haud off," and then said to me. "I'll push from behind, and just remember no one passes Margaret Pendleton. Now heave, you lummox."

I dragged sleds for five hours. Somewhere around noon, work stopped for what was called "baggin." Never had food been so welcome. There was a thick piece of cheese and a chunk of brown bread, and wonder of wonders, a large flat custard pie.

"Don't think tha'll get custard pie every day," said Peg. "We get custard only when the cows and heifers calve. This is a gift from 'is grace's dairyman. Beast milk makes the best custard, and he's sweet on Ma."

Minutes later, it seemed, I was back in harness. Peg had decided I could be trusted to work alone. Once I overheard her talking with Tom when I returned from the sough.

"He's a likely lad, Peg," Tom was saying, "and a

right educated one by the way he talks."

"He ain't no half a man."

"Peg," replied the hewer, puffing his pipe, "he's never been in a pit before. Does tha remember what you were like when tha came down for the first time? Tha was skriking all day."

"I was not!"

"Tha was. But look at thee now. Seems to me you're a bit sweet on that lad."

"I'm not. He's such a girt fool."

"Only in a mine, Peg. That lad—" He took up his pipe from his mouth and laid it aside. "That lad, for all he's not yet fifteen, still likely knows more o' t'world than I do at thrice his age. Would tha want to marry a collier and live all yer life in Worsley afearing each day a cave-in or an explosion of the firedamp?"

"Well, he ain't done so bad with the sleds. I'll say that."

"And 'e's a good-looking lad, Peg. Plenty girls around 'ere be glad to work alongside of him. Anyhows I think tha's sweet on him."

There was the sound of a lump of coal hitting the wall, a laugh from Tom and then the sound of a pick splintering coal.

Tom and Joe left soon after. The hewer spoke to me first. "I've left you two enough for a couple of more hours. I don't want you to do too much this first day."

He placed his hand on my shoulder. "George, tha's done a fine day's work. There's plenty can't stand being in a coal pit. They gets the trembles so bad just at the thought of all that mountain above. That's nowt to be ashamed of. I'd rather work with someone who's scared than a fool. Happen I'll see the duke soon, and I'll tell 'im tha's given a good account of thysel'."

I felt so happy, I could have kissed his feet for joy.

The last two hours were an eternity. We labored on. Sled after sled went down to the landing stage and hundredweight after hundredweight of coal was tipped into the narrow boats and floated out.

Finally, when I could scarce move a muscle, Peg declared herself satisfied.

"Come on," she said, "that's enough for today, let's leave some for tomorrow."

I said nothing, I was too exhausted to speak.

"That's a joke," she added. "Tha's no sense o'humor, hast tha?"

How I got out of the mine I'll never know. The light outside almost blinded me, and there wasn't a muscle that didn't ache. My hands and knees were rubbed raw. Fingernails were broken off and across my body, where the belt had fitted, there was a deep purple welt. I was coal black from matted hair to blistered feet. My back would not straighten until we were halfway up Mill Brow.

"Come on," said her highness, "I'm hungry."

All I wanted to do was crawl into bed, but when we reached the cottage, Peg striding up the hill, me hobbling like a hunchback behind, we found that Mrs. Pendleton

had the large tin bathtub ready and was boiling a caul-
dron of water on the fire.

"Peg, you'll have to wait 'til George has finished,
then use the same water. I'll keep the kettle on t'hob."

I couldn't follow much of what was said after that.
Peg and her mother argued back and forth for some ten
minutes in such strange Lancashire talk that most of it
escaped me. There was no mistaking the meaning, however. I also caught the phrase "half a man" several times.

Mrs. Pendleton carried the day, the tub was mine.
The daughter glared at me. "Well, I hope tha's satisfied."

"It seems to me," I said, choosing my words carefully, "that a compromise is possible."

"Oh Gawd, a compromise," said Peg, coming very
near to my accent and manner of speaking, "a compromise is possible."

"We work six days a week," I went on. "I could use
the tub first on Tuesday, Thursday and Saturday, Peg on
the other three days."

There was complete silence. Both women stared at
me open-mouthed.

"That sounds fair to me," said Mrs. Pendleton, "what
do you say to that, Peg?"

"Seems all right," admitted the daughter. "Then I go
first tonight," she added with satisfaction.

Her mother began to say something to me, but I was
fast asleep on my bed, coal dust and all.

CHAPTER · 5

Noah's Flood

My second day in the duke's mine went no easier than the first, but Black Tom praised me and told me I was a "likely lad," which didn't please Miss Margaret Pendleton.

"Half-a-man" she complained, "the duke's taken boggarts."

On Friday morning, just as I was about to leave for the mine, the duke sent his valet, Aubrey, to the cottage.

"His grace wants thee," he said, "at road."

When I reached the basin, the duke greeted me warmly. He stood gazing at the water coming from the mine.

"I want you to meet my agent, Mr. Gilbert. He'll be here by and by." He looked back at the yellow water.

"I suppose you've heard about the sough?" he asked. "Well it's not deep enough. Ah!" he added, smiling, "a rhyme—'sough' and 'enough'. I like that. Though Lord knows, 'tis scarcely a subject for jest."

He paused, then added, "Without it this mine is

doomed. 'Tis a miracle no one has been drowned long since. In a few weeks, 'twill have silted up and flooded all the new seams. If I build a new one it will cost more than the mine produces; if I don't Worsley will die."

Turning to me, he said, "This village is my life; I shan't marry. The lady I carried a torch for married someone less, er, less . . . eccentric."

He glanced upward. Mist no longer obscured the top of the sandstone cliff, which rose a hundred feet above the quarry and the basin.

Reaching for his snuff box, he took out a large pinch. Thrusting the powder to his nose, he gave several short, vigorous snorts. A loud sneeze followed, then two more, and the tears had scarcely cleared from his eyes when he observed a miner crossing the common. As he drew close, the duke hailed him.

"What, Roger, 'tis a little after your hour, is it not?"

"Indeed it is, your grace," replied the man with a slight bow. "But I was up all night with my wife who was safe delivered of twin boys this very day."

"Capital, capital," replied the duke. "We must be grateful for what the good lord sends us."

"Aye, right enough, your grace. But a notices as how he sends all t'babbies to our house an t'gold to thine!"

At this the duke laughed and fished in his waistcoat pocket producing a guinea. "Well, take this and drink my health at the Grapes tonight."

"Thank you, your grace," said the man, and pocketing the coin, he touched his forelock and waded up the sough into the mine.

The duke turned back to me. "Icarus, you've made a good start here. I've a mind to keep you with me awhile longer. There's a real shortage of intelligent, reliable people. And you've settled in right nicely. 'Tis not the sort of place that takes to strangers gladly. Black Tom thinks very highly of you, and he's a shrewd judge. For a while longer, you must win coal. No help for that. But soon I may have need of someone to keep track of my brass. The only people who can add and spell are all strangers, the locals don't trust 'em."

"I'll do my best, your grace."

"I know you will. As for casting up my accounts, I can teach you. Honesty's the main thing. The men must have an absolute trust in you. Even the slightest mistake and it's the basin for thee, or worse." He chuckled and looked into the yellow water. "That's human nature I suppose. D'ye know why I took a liking to you, lad, from the first?"

"No, sir."

"Instinct, Icarus, instinct. I trust my instincts. Of course, I have excellent advisors, the best in England, but when all's said and done, I trust to instinct.

"I also want you to know that I've made what inquiries I can on your behalf. A certain traveling actor made a guinea from one of my agents for telling no more of your life than you yourself told me."

"That would be Mr. Winstone."

"Well, he was a rare talker from all I could gather. Should ought else be discovered, I'll let you know."

"Thank you, your grace."

We saw a man hurrying across the common on foot.

"In the mean time, Icarus, there's a place here for you—if you can delve in yonder pit!"

"Thank you, your—"

"Nay, no thanks. Reward me with loyalty. Ah! Here's Gilbert."

The agent raised his hat in greeting. "Good morning, your grace."

"Morning, John. This is the young man you helped me fish out of Worsley Basin."

We shook hands.

"There's no time for formalities now," said the duke. "I must have your news, John."

I had a chance to study the agent while he talked with his employer. He was older and a little taller than the duke and only slightly more stylish in his dress and manner, though he wore a lace cravat and a dark blue waistcoat.

"I talked with Lord Strange, your grace, as instructed."

"And?"

"He speaks for all the proprietors of the Mersey and Irwell Navigation—they will not ship your grace's pit coals at less than twelve shillings a ton."

"Twelve shillings! That will more than double the price, and I must still carry them by packhorse to the River Irwell."

"Aye, your grace. I believe Lord Strange and the other proprietors mean to hold you to ransom."

"The devil take them," replied the duke. "They have

a monopoly of trade on the River Irwell, yet they have made no improvements. A man may wait a month for them to carry his coals, and yet they want to charge the full rate."

"Well, we can continue as before with carts and horses, your grace."

"Aye, John, we can." He slapped his thigh in frustration. "But then the poor of Manchester must pay two shillings for a load, while here at the pit 'tis only ten pence. Coal costs more to carry than it does to get. D'ye have the figures I asked for?"

Mr. Gilbert reached into his coat pocket and produced a sheet of neatly written numbers. The duke studied them for several minutes.

"So 'tis as we thought."

"Aye, your grace. There is enough coal under Walkden Moor to make you one of the richest men in England. There's even some, not a great lot, of cannel coal, but unless it can be transported to Manchester or Liverpool in some cheaper fashion you'll not profit from it."

The agent produced a second sheet of paper. "I believe the best coal lies to the north of Shaving Lane Fault, pretty much under Walkden Moor. There may be four or five seams below Seven Feet Seam."

The duke studied the paper. "Then we must have a new drain at surface level. How far is that above sea level, John?"

"Eighty-two feet, and t'will cost your grace a pretty penny."

"Pennies I would gladly give, but this will be

pounds, but if I don't do it, Worsley will be destroyed, for there's nowt else to do hereabouts." He looked at the paper again, sighed and said, "How many men do I employ, John?"

"Over a hundred, your grace, counting the lads and lasses."

"And what do I pay them, on the average, I mean?"

"Six shillings for a miner, half that for a woman, boys under ten an eighth, lads over ten count as a quarter man, and at fifteen, a half man. Lassies pretty much the same if they work hard."

"A clever system, eh John?"

" 'Tis more than generous, your grace."

"D'ye think so? Well."

He hesitated, as if this thought was new to him. "But if it is in my power to help others and benefit myself why should I not be generous? 'Tis the duty, aye, the duty, of those who rule to provide for those not so blessed."

He looked up at us. "I'm no ranting preacher, but I suffered enough in my childhood to have sympathy for the underdog. All my six brothers dead, the persecutions of my stepfather, the absence of my mother, these almost drove me to despair."

He turned away, as if embarrassed, and aware he had said more than he intended. For a long time he gazed at the mouth of the sough, then he reached for his snuffbox.

"To think," he said, more to himself than to us,

"there are those who deny the medicinal qualities of snuff. They say pulverized tobacco cannot be good for the body. They are wrong, wrong! Wrong! I was very poorly as a child; some thought me daft in the head. Well, look at me now. Did you know that two Popes threatened excommunication to anyone taking snuff?" he asked us.

"No, your grace, I didn't," replied Mr. Gilbert.

"Of course, the Church of England was ne'er so barbaric. Dost tha care for a pinch?"

"Thank you, but no," said the agent hastily.

"Well then," replied his employer, taking a large pinch between thumb and forefinger and hoisting it up to his nose. A series of loud snorts followed.

The duke's head reared back and then jerked forward with an explosion like the discharge of a gun.

Mr. Gilbert had the greatest difficulty keeping a straight face. He spoke to me, more I think to distract himself than because he sought information.

"How do you find the work, George?" he asked.

" 'Tis hard, sir, and several things puzzle me."

"Indeed?" said the duke putting his snuff box away, "for example?"

"Well, sir, all day long I drag sleds from the stall to the sough. But a boat can carry several tons of coal and only one person has to pole it. The water flows out of the mine and carries the boat with it."

"Well, it's a matter of displacement and current, lad," said Mr. Gilbert, "though I scarce expect you to understand."

"But if his grace builds a new drain, as he must or lose the mine . . ."

"Aye, I must," muttered the duke, "though 'tis hardly a new thought."

"Why not build it much bigger, big enough to bear the coal boats right to the place where the hewers work? Then the coal can be put directly into the boats, and there would be no need to drag the sleds."

"Poor Icarus," said the duke sorrowfully, "the blow to his head has quite addled his brains."

"And," I added, stung by this, "since the coal is already on barges why not extend the sough all the way to Liverpool and Manchester and save horses and toll roads."

"The lad's mad," roared his grace, "he must be confined. Water is taken out of a mine, not put in it. The boy would drown us all."

"But your grace," said Mr. Gilbert, "the idea of a navigation, or even a canal, is not new. There is one nearby at Sankey Brook."

"Aye, aye, Gilbert, but didst ever hear of a canal in a coal mine?"

"No, your grace, that I did not."

"Well, that's my point. The Sankey navigation is one thing, what Icarus here suggests is another dose of Noah's flood. It's clear he's no miner so I shall have to put him in charge of my accounts. That way he can't flood my mine or drown my colliers."

So saying he left, and the only comfort I had was a broad wink from his grace's agent.

CHAPTER · 6

The Duke's Canal

That night I had the dream again. It began as I lay trying to sleep on the straw pallet that served as a mattress. Outside, the clock struck two, and then for a long time there was silence broken only occasionally by the mournful hoot of an owl. Now life stands still, and I am suddenly outside time, an observer watching my own nightmare, fascinated by terror, incapable of stopping it.

I stand guarded in a large dark room. At the far end stands a great oak table on a raised platform. Sitting behind the desk is a man dressed in black with a long white powdered wig.

Over his eyes is a narrow black bandage. He rises to his feet pointing a thin wooden switch in my direction.

The cart draws up a long hill. I stand alone, my elbows pinioned to my side. The horse slowly edges its way through crowds of people dressed in holiday attire. All seem to be shouting, but I hear no sounds.

As the cart climbs the hill, a wooden platform comes

into view. Rising above it are two huge wooden posts with a beam across them.

A small, wiry man with dark piercing eyes comes toward me; in his hands is a black cap, which he places over my face. A rope tightens around my neck.

There is a long pause. I kick off my shoes; then the ground opens beneath my feet. I am falling into a black chasm. The rope burns around my neck. I cannot breathe; my arms thrash madly as I gasp for air.

"Wake up George. Wake up."

I was sitting bolt upright in bed, my teeth chattering, shivering and trembling. Sweat had soaked the bed sheet.

By the curtain stood Peg, a stub of candle in her hand. Her face was white. Mrs. Pendleton was shaking me by the shoulder.

"George, wake up! You've been having that nightmare again, haven't you?"

"Yes, for I will swear I was to be hanged. For some reason a man with a bandage over his eyes wishes me dead."

I lay back in bed, gasping for breath. "Nay. 'Tis not the first time I've dreamed such a dream, but never has it gone on so long or seemed so real. It was as if I could reach out and touch the people, though who they are and why they should wish me dead, I know not.

"It is as if the corner of a veil was lifted. I have seen that man before, but where or how . . ."

" 'Tis only a dream," said Peg. "Come, Ma. It will be morning soon enough."

And with that they left me. But there was no sleep for me that night, and it was a relief when I heard the knocker-up coming rapidly up Mill Brow, knocking on doors and singing out, "Rise up, by God, and get to work."

I was now a familiar enough figure in Worsley. Word of my meeting with the duke had spread rapidly among the colliers. I was the butt of many a good-natured jest for days after. In particular, my idea for driving the canal to the headings caused a great deal of merriment, and some miners thought it great sport to call me Noah.

Of course, there were those who resented my presence; they were few in number and about my age. One great lout in particular told me to stay away from Peg. "She's t' be my lass, and don't tha forget it."

Long after others had tired of the sport, one or two would loosen some of the hazel twigs in the bottom of a basket. When I began dragging it, the coal would spill out as I fell on my face. Another trick was to file the cat-band on a sled so that my chain sprang loose and struck me a wicked blow on the back.

Peg's admirer was the worst of the lot, but I found a way to deal with him. One day, I came upon a basket he had prepared for me. I slipped it into Peg's pile. As she was dragging it to the sled, the coal fell out on the main road, and he began laughing in his tunnel imagining my discomfort. Miss Margaret Pendleton went straight into his heading with a large piece of coal, which, to judge by the howls, she smashed to dust on his thick skull. After that, no one bothered me again.

At the end of the third week, the Pendletons and I were sitting in the cottage by the fire when a messenger arrived to say I was to wait upon the duke at the Hall. It lay only half a mile from our cottage. I hurried up the lane and quickly crossed the stone flags of the courtyard. The building seemed strangely designed. Two wings jutted out on each side of the courtyard and certain rooms appeared to have been added on as afterthoughts. Four massive sets of chimneys poked up into a cloud of dirty black smoke.

The front door was scarcely imposing being rather narrow and lacking any kind of portico to shelter guests in the event of rain. Two very small narrow windows of thick green glass were set in dark wood that bore unmistakable traces of soot.

To my right was a rusty bell pull, which I yanked on vigorously. Far away I heard the sound of a cracked bell, and it was some considerable time before a footman answered. He was dressed in blue and silver livery, somewhat threadbare in places. Obviously his wig had recently been powdered. Despite the bag, there was flour all over his coat.

He was appalled at my insolence.

"Round to the servants' entrance," he ordered in shocked tones. "The very idea, a pit boy at the front entrance."

"His grace has sent for me," I said, determined to put the fellow in his place. "If you do not admit me, I shall return home, and you can answer to him."

His eyes started from his head like a prawn's.

"You damn guttersnipe, I'll tak' my belt to your hide."

At this moment, the duke himself appeared, demanding to know what the ruckus was.

"Pit boy, your grace, at the front door."

"Come in, Icarus," said the duke. Then he turned to the footman. "Mind you treat him and those like him civilly. For their labor pays thy wages, and don't tha forget it."

The servant moved aside, still glowering, and the duke led me across a noble hall floored with black and white marble squares and ushered me into an elegantly paneled room. "I'm sorry about that, Icarus," he said. "Though I took the fellow on in Bolton, he has the manners of a London servant on board wages."

Mr. Gilbert was seated in the room, which I now saw was a library. Four or five oak bookcases stuffed with books and adorned with graceful moldings had been pushed to the far side of the room. Large pictures of the duke's ancestors gazed sternly down. There was a writing desk and inkstand, an easy chair covered with leather and a pair of steps. From the ceiling, wreathed in tobacco smoke, hung two brass chandeliers.

A fire spluttered in the grate. It seemed the duke's coal was no better than our own, and on the mantelpiece lay several pipes and a large jar of tobacco. In the center of the room was a long table spread with papers. Mr. Gilbert sat by this, his pipe also alight. The smoke filled my lungs, and I coughed.

"Aye, aye," muttered the duke, "open a window, will you, Gilbert."

The agent smiled, rose and pushed open two of the small mullioned windows.

"I like a pipe indoors, and snuff out. If you're to stay in Worsley, Icarus, you must get used to it."

A small table next to the fireplace had a silver punch bowl and glasses on it. "Do you care for some punch?"

"Thank you, no."

He poured himself a glass. Mr. Gilbert also took one. "Do ye know what this is, Icarus?" he asked, walking to the table and pointing to one of the papers.

I studied it carefully. "It is a map of Lancashire," I replied.

"Aye, that it is. Don't seem so surprised that I should ask thee, for I'll wager no one in Worsley has seen one."

"Do you see Worsley, George?" asked Mr. Gilbert.

"Yes, I do."

"And the River Irwell?"

"Yes."

"Well," continued the agent, "his grace has been thinking of your plan to dig a canal from the mine to Manchester. The canal could go to the River Irwell and then link with the Irwell Navigation to Manchester."

I felt a surge of pride. So my idea was not so foolish after all.

The duke pointed with the stem of his pipe. "You see the River Irwell is navigable, or at least it could be if the company looked to their responsibilities. Of course, what you propose is quite different."

"I don't follow, your grace."

"Some years ago," he said, knocking his pipe out in the fire and reaching down the tobacco jar, "I toured Europe. So I know what a lot of men don't. 'Tis possible to make a water road where nature never intended. A canal is man-made; a navigation is an improvement on what nature hath wrought."

He stuffed tobacco into the bowl of his pipe, took a taper and puffed contentedly.

"Now," he said. "You are proposing a canal. We would have to start from nothing; we may not be able to find a single man who knows anything of digging canals or of building locks.

"Locks? Why locks, your grace? Surely no one can steal a canal?"

"Nay, lad"—he coughed several times—"I don't mean those kinds of locks. In a canal, the water must be almost level, with just a slow flow from its highest point down to the sea. Worsley is thirty odd feet above the River Irwell. Our boats will have to be lowered down by at least five locks. It can be done, but no one in England has ever done it, and locks use a devil of a lot of water.

"However," he continued, sitting in the leather easy chair. "Gilbert and I are prepared to admit that your plan may have merit." He looked at Mr. Gilbert, who puffed on his pipe and nodded his agreement.

"The French have enjoyed the advantages of the Canal du Midi for over fifty years." He paused and signaled Mr. Gilbert to pour him a second glass of port. "Even the best horse can only pull two tons on a good road. But that same horse can tow almost a hundred tons on water."

He took a long drink. "God knows where the money will come from to carry a canal seven miles across open country. It might cost as much as a thousand guineas a mile. Think o' that! Seven thousand guineas."

"It could be more, your grace," said his agent.

"Aye, mayhap." The duke drew indignantly on his pipe.

"What about my idea of driving the canal along the coal face?" I ventured.

"Madness!" roared the duke, "tha takes water *out* of a mine, not puts it in."

I left a few minutes later with no regrets. The truth was my eyes were watering and I couldn't see anything for tobacco smoke.

CHAPTER · 7

The First Act

Several days passed and I heard nothing more—though it was rumored that the duke and Mr. Gilbert were up to "summat." As for me, I continued to drag sleds, and when the shift was over I was happy to eat supper and crawl into bed.

March became April; the days grew longer, and we left the mine in daylight. The frost was out of the ground; carts and horses loaded with coal sank into the soggy ground or became stuck in oozy mud.

Often we stumbled into the mine chilled to the bone with driving rains. At other times we hurried home as a late-day shower soaked coal dust deep into our hair and clothes.

Peg's attitude toward me didn't change much, yet everyone felt she was sweet on me. "Tha's lucky, lad," one hewer said to me, "for she's the prettiest lass round these parts."

I thought about that all day, and that night I let her

use the tub first even though it was a Thursday. After I had taken my turn and poured the water away in the back yard, I sat by the fire with Peg and her mother. I looked at her very closely as she sat carding wool.

"Do you ever wonder about your parents, George?" asked Mrs. Pendleton.

"Often," I admitted. "Though Mr. Winstone and his family reared me, and I consider them my greatest friends, I still wonder about my true parents. I mean . . ."

"Go on George," she said.

"I wonder about them. I would so like to meet them. To know them. To discover why they gave me up."

"I can scarcely recall Pa," said Peg. "I was but five when he was killed in Wood Pit."

Just then our eyes met and Peg's face turned brick red. I looked away quickly. "Better get to bed," I muttered, feeling very foolish. "It will be morning soon enough."

"Good night, George," said her mother who was looking as pleased as a cat who had swallowed a pint of cream.

"Good night," I replied, taking a final look at her daughter who was now savagely poking at the smoky fire.

On April 16, leaflets began appearing in Worsley, Walkden, and the surrounding villages. The few that could read soon spread the word to those that couldn't. The same message was printed in the *Manchester Mercury* and read from pulpits in dozens of churches.

NOTICE! NOTICE!

HIS GRACE, FRANCIS, THIRD DUKE OF BRIDGE-
WATER, HAS PETITIONED PARLIAMENT AND
BEEN GRANTED AN ACT TO MAKE A NAVIGABLE
CUT BETWEEN A PLACE IN WORSLEY CALLED THE
DELPH AND THE RIVER IRWELL.

ALL SOBER, HARD-WORKING PERSONS POS-
SESSING SKILLS IN BLACK-SMITHING, QUAR-
RYING, MINING, BOATBUILDING, CARPENTRY,
MASONRY, ETC. SHOULD MAKE APPLICATION TO
MR. JOHN GILBERT, HIS GRACE'S AGENT. THEY
WILL BE ASSURED OF THE MOST CONSIDERATE
ATTENTION.

SIGNED
Bridgewater

Some miners were taken from the pit and put to other tasks. A works' yard had to be constructed, and most of the common at Worsley was fenced in. A large chimney was begun by Mr. Bridges and his son Peter, our local masons.

By the end of April no beds were left in Worsley or Walkden. Men were lodged as far away as Bolton in the north and Leigh in the west. Carts brought them in early each morning and bore their exhausted bodies home at night.

Peg and I were taken out of the mine and given other tasks, and I was not sorry. Neither was Peg, but she was too proud to say so. She carried messages from the duke and his agent to various foremen. I was given a ledger in which the hours of work were recorded and wages cast up.

The duke had a large table with an awning over it placed by the mill. There he and Mr. Gilbert studied maps and drew up their plans.

A team of fifty laborers, some of whom were French and Dutch, began to enlarge the basin below the cliff where I had made my dramatic entry into the duke's affairs.

Besides the canal there was the new sough to be built. It was to be well below the old one and on a level with the proposed canal.

"The canal will be eighty-two feet above the sea level, George," he said, "and it will gradually slope toward the Irwell. The sough will head directly north and be eight feet high and ten wide. Soon you'll see headings that have been under water for months become dry.

"There won't be much mining for a while, too much blasting." He grinned and clamped his hat on his head. "Now I've to tell Black Tom he's to dig in the mud awhile. You're lucky to be here figuring wages."

A boat yard sprang up. Richard Lomax, the master boat builder, and John Lloyd, a Welshman from Rhyl, began work on special boats to carry materials down the canal to the diggers. They called them flats. Each could carry a dozen men or a great pile of supplies along the surface canal.

Even at night work continued. Torches of tow and pitch were fixed upon poles so that men had enough light to dig by. From the enlarged basin, the sough drove north into the sandstone mountain. In the other direction, the yellow serpent wound past the mill toward the River Irwell, some seven miles distant. Rows of wooden pegs with small flannel flags marked the first two miles of the route.

Men who were at first astonished, even fearful, of the bright yellow water leaching from the mine, now stripped to their drawers to dig in the slimy earth.

"Well, Icarus," said the duke to me one day, "see what you have wrought."

Everywhere I looked men labored. There was the sound of blasting now as the new sough was driven through the rock. Half a mile away, the laborers carved a river through the earth. Strange devices called wheelbarrows were much used. They were filled with earth and then pushed along planks on a single wheel to where the soil was heaped to form a canal bank.

" 'Tis like the building of the pyramids," said the duke.

"Pyramids, your grace?"

"Aye, Icarus, the tombs of the ancient kings of Egypt. 'Tis all that is remembered of them now, and mayhap this canal will be all that men will recall of us, too."

I quickly learned to cast up accounts. The duke's interests were vast, but I was concerned with the mine and canal only. Few, if any, envied my rise from drawer to accounts keeper. Indeed, one day Black Tom told me he had rather draw sleds himself than argue fines on pay Saturday. In truth, it was no fun to tell a grown man that he was to get less than he thought. However, I stuck to my guns, and no one carried out his threat to "pitch me in t'basin."

In all difficult matters, Mr. Gilbert, the duke's agent, was an eager source of help. He was a self-effacing person who did much, but sought no praise. The duke himself assured me that if I modeled myself on Gilbert I would have nought to fear in this world or the next. There was no job that the agent could not do, but like the rest of us, he had no experience of building a canal. He stayed up late at night with the duke pouring over charts and sketches, leaving only when he was too tired to read. But he remained always cheerful. When things went wrong, he was first on the scene, exhorting and encouraging the men.

One day I was adding up columns of figures at the duke's table while he studied the latest surveys of Mr. Gilbert. A group of men left the sough and approached us.

The duke straightened up when he saw them and addressed them.

"Well, lads, is this a deputation, or are ye done for the day?"

There was some shuffling of feet, and finally one of them spoke for all.

"It's the new sough, your grace. It's hit solid rock now."

"Yes?"

"The lads here feel 'tis waste of time tryin' to dig through the rock."

The duke's eyes flashed fire.

"So you and the lads think that, do ye?"

Several of them nodded, and a couple murmured, "Aye."

The spokesman went on hurriedly. "O' course 'tis your grace's brass we gets paid with, but we can't make our lot through t'hard stuff. At this rate we shall get but three shillings a week."

The duke reached into his pocket for his gold snuff box. "And ye have combined to make a strike, eh?"

"Nay, nay, your grace," said the leader, "there's nay talk o' a strike."

"I'm relieved to hear it," said the duke grimly, "for workers will not combine on my land. Now do ye see this pinch of snuff?"

He took a tiny amount between finger and thumb.

Several men nodded. "Do ye think ye can get this much rock out today?"

"Aye."

"Then do so."

Sullenly they turned to go. "And," continued the duke, "I'll see ye get paid your regular amount for going through the hard stuff."

All unhappy looks vanished, and the men crossed the bridge and waded happily up into the sough.

His grace sighed. " 'Tis a heavy responsibility being a duke. Now I must pay them six shillings a yard instead of for two yards. I should buy the Grapes, for all my brass is spent there."

He brooded for a while, then said, "Icarus, make a note of the new rate for going through the hard stuff and make sure you add 'to be paid back when going through the soft stuff.' "

But the duke's troubles were not over. Later he was standing on the swing bridge when Peg came by carrying a huge bundle of loose wool cardings in her arms. She didn't see the duke, and he didn't see her until she bounced off him. There was a roar of anger from his grace as he disappeared under the load. Wool flew everywhere. The commotion brought workers running from all directions. Those who had hats flapped them vigorously in hope of scattering the fluff from their enraged employer. It only made matters worse, and the Third Duke of Bridgewater took on the appearance of a large two-legged sheep. Peg turned her head, fairly exploding with suppressed laughter.

The duke tried to get the last laugh, though. The next day a sign was erected by the bridge. On it was etched in white letters:

THIS BRIDGE IS CLOSED TO ALL FEMALES WITH BURDENS.

Bridgewater

Nobody paid any attention to it.

Schemer Brindley

Worsley, once a quiet country village, now took on the appearance of an army camp. To the north, under the sheer sandstone cliff, men blasted and hacked and drove the sough underground, foot by foot.

The use of gunpowder severely hampered the coal mining operation, for no one could be below ground when powder was exploded. The duke fretted at this, for when no coal was got his income ceased. "A navigation should have coals at the heels of it," he said on more than one occasion. This saying became something of a joke with the men.

The common suffered most. Not only had it been fenced in to form the works' yard, but the brook was culverted and made to flow twenty feet below the ground.

A Mrs. Perkins was put in charge of an outdoor kitchen. Since many men lived ten miles away, there was a need to feed them at midday.

"It will cost me a lot of brass, Icarus," said the duke

looking across the common at the kitchen, "but happy men work harder, and it may be worth it in the long run."

I doubt there was a sight like it in all England. Crowds of men sitting at two tables under a huge awning outside the cottage that served as the kitchen.

Inside Mrs. Perkins bustled around supervising four undercooks who were known as the four Marys. She was a little birdlike creature who always dressed in a plain loose gown and lace butterfly cap. She was a fearful person when roused. One day a miner criticized a custard tart, and she poured a pan of red hot drippings over him. Even his grace tested the winds before intruding on her.

"She's a true artist, Icarus," he told me one day. "Such people are rare in the history of the world, and I tell ye frankly, I'd rather have one of her cherry tarts than those dreary Italian paintings that are so much in vogue. I prefer native talent to foreign—in all things. All true Englishmen do."

The kitchen was a hive of industry, though occasionally I ventured to sit beside the roaring fire and sip a glass of cider or chew on a large slice of freshly baked bread and a piece of Cheshire cheese.

In addition to the open fireplace, there were two Dutch ovens. The chimney was hung with bacon and the rack that covered half the ceiling creaked under its burden of cured hams, salt pork, and black puddings. 'Twas said some came to the kitchen just to smell the air. Mrs. Perkins made a delicious local pastry called Lancashire fat rascals. Whenever I caught wind of rascals baking, I found some flimsy pretext to consult with her.

Little was left to chance; his grace prowled everywhere. When he discovered that many of the men caught severe colds from working up to their waists in freezing water, he ordered honey and coltsfoot to be made into a hot drink. This successfully loosened the tightest coughs, and the men soon returned to their duty.

The sough progressed in fits and starts because of the difference in rock strata, but the overland canal moved steadily forward. The first half mile was soon completed, and Mr. Lomax and the other boat builders added sails to the flats so that the wind could help move them down the canal. When nature failed, the men hauled the boats by hand or used two mules borrowed from Manor House Farm.

New types of boats were needed in the mine. These craft were long and narrow and designed to carry eight tons of coal without drawing more than a foot of water. Mr. Lomax looked at them one day and said, "Tall and very thin, they look like starving men." From that day on, the boats were called "starvationers."

The cold and damp disappeared as April became May. Now the torment was flies and biting insects. There was an outbreak of fever, but still the work progressed.

Mr. Gilbert moved to Worsley on Midsummer's Day, 1759. I was helping him unload his furniture when the duke's carriage pulled up at the door.

"Good morning to ye both," said the duke, mopping

his face with a handkerchief and waving his carriage away. "A warm one, too. I'll rest here with your permission."

" 'Tis indeed, your grace," replied his agent. "But we must 'take advantage of it; 'twill be winter soon enough."

"Aye, aye," muttered his grace, "then it will cost me, I'll warrant." He sat on a large wicker hamper.

"I fear rain more, your grace, for if the water rises it may sweep away a bank into the next county."

"That's why I called on you, John. I've been to the canal, and I care little for what I hear. There was a bank burst this morning, and it's not the first time it has happened. But see, John, no reflection on you, but we must find help, someone who knows canals. I have in mind to send to France for an engineer skilled in such matters."

The agent looked thoughtful for a moment, then sat on a box opposite the duke.

"Begging your grace's pardon, I doubt the wisdom of that."

The duke reached for his pipe, and there was a pause while his agent rummaged through his effects to find his tobacco jar. "Well then." He sighed. "What's to be done? For as you know, I'll do nothing without your say so."

"I appreciate your grace's confidence. I've been thinking of an engineer who has worked for your guardian, Earl Gower. You may well have heard of him—James Brindley, the wheelwright."

The duke considered this for a few moments, puffing gently on his clay. "He has done nothing with canals, but then who has? I know of the man. They call him 'the schemer' and say he made water flow uphill when he drained Heathcote's Gal Pit at Clifton Colliery."

" 'Twas a brilliant solution, your grace, and by using a siphon he did seem to make water flow uphill."

"This Brindley is a rough diamond for all I hear, John."

At that instant I thought I saw the trace of a smile on Mr. Gilbert's face, but the duke didn't notice. "I'll send for him. I suppose it'll cost me."

"I'm certain, your grace, he'll be worth the expense."

"I hope so, for this scheme is costing me a fortune and no end in sight. Likely I shall owe twenty thousand guineas before we're done. But now I'll take my leave. I thought I caught the aroma of baked apple dumplings as I passed the kitchen."

On July 1, I received an order to present myself at the Hall at eight o'clock. By great good fortune, it was my turn to have the warm water first. Mrs. Pendleton and I were very curious about the summons and so was her daughter, though she pretended not to be.

Once again I went boldly to the front door. The footman glared but admitted me.

"Follow me, and keep yer 'ands off things," he said.

I was shown into the library. All the windows were open, but a familiar cloud of smoke was settling about the low ceiling. The oak table was covered with papers as usual. On top of them was perched a decanter of port.

The duke was leaning on the mantelpiece, a long

churchwarden pipe in his mouth. Mr. Gilbert was sitting in the leather armchair wearing his usual silk cravat though it was uncomfortably hot in the room.

Mr. Brindley, for it could only be he, stood by the table, a cherrywood pipe in his mouth. We shook hands solemnly enough, though I caught a twinkle in his eye.

He wore a neatly tied cravat and a well-cut, though old, snuff-colored coat. The white waistcoat covered an ample stomach. His hands were large and rough.

"So ye're the lad who suggested the idea of a canal?"

He did not speak like a Lancashire man.

"Yes, sir."

"Lad, we'll do better if ye call me Mr. Brindley. We Derbyshire men care little for titles, right, duke?"

His grace, the Third Duke of Bridgewater, who had probably never been called simply "duke" in all his twenty-three years of life, managed a weak, "Aye, aye, Brindley."

"The duke here," said the engineer, "agrees with me that your idea can be improved upon somewhat."

"Yes, yes," his grace put in hurriedly, "but perhaps this—"

"My idea, George," continued Mr. Brindley, as if the duke didn't exist, "is to extend the canal up the sough and right up to the headings and float the coal out in boats. That way the water does all the work."

"But Mr. Brindley," I said, glaring at my employer who was very carefully studying a piece of paper, though he held it upside down, "surely you take water out of a mine, not bring it in?"

"Lad, new challenges mean new approaches. The duke saw that right away when I put it to him, didn't you, duke?"

"Aye, aye, Brindley." There was a spluttering sound from Mr. Gilbert.

"Now," said the engineer, turning to me and blowing a cloud of smoke to the ceiling. "I'm going to need someone to work for me. Make notes, write letters, that kind of thing. Can you do it as well as the accounts and fines?"

"I think so."

Mr. Brindley reached for a canvas bag lying on the armchair. He rooted through its contents. I saw a Bible and a prayer book.

"Ah," he said, "a present for you, George, at the beginning of our partnership."

He held up two delicately carved wooden watermills. "Carve them myself," he said. "Not much to it."

The duke and his agent came over and examined one while I looked at the other.

"I've never seen workmanship like it," said the duke in awe. "Why, even the waterwheel turns."

"And, your grace, if you peep through the door you will see the wheel turns a drive shaft that moves the grindstones inside," added Mr. Gilbert.

"Incredible," breathed the duke; "I never saw the like. 'Tis worth all that so-called art I sent back during my

Grand Tour. Brindley, can I have the other one?"

Brindley blushed. "Aye, aye, duke. 'Tis nought but a way of filling time. And now, if ye'll pass me that box of Fribourg and Treyer's exotic mixture, we can get down to business."

We did get down, quite literally. Mr. Brindley liked to sketch with a lump of chalk on the floor.

"I've already made an ocular survey of the route," said the engineer, drawing a line on the floor. "It's a good one, John, nice and straight, but we'll save a lot of trouble by following a slightly different way. There'll be some bends and a bit o' winding, but we can stick to the eighty-two foot contour."

"But Brindley," said the duke in alarm, "that will mean an extra mile or two. Think of the cost."

"Duke," he said kindly, "I'm thinking of the cost. A lock will cost more than two miles of digging. And anyway, our biggest problem is finding water."

"What about the let-leases from the mine?" I suggested. "There's plenty of that."

"Aye, maybe plenty in Worsely, but by the time we reach the Irwell, we'll be down to about one foot of water. And then the locks down to the level of the Irwell will require huge amounts. Just to lower a boat eight feet uses over a hundred tons of water."

There was a sharp intake of breath by Mr. Gilbert.

"We'll need at least three reservoirs, and work will have to begin on digging one on Walkden Moor because the undergound canal will soon need more water."

He stood up and slapped chalk dust from his breeches. "Duke, it will be costly. Not less than ten thousand guineas a year. Can you afford it?"

I had expected the duke to explode at this news, but he did not. Instead, he picked up a piece of paper.

"Brindley, I don't know, and that's the truth. I shall cut my expenses to four hundred pounds a year and borrow what I can. I won't sell my land; anyway so much of it is entailed I couldn't mortgage it if I wanted to. But I'm determined to make the attempt. Are ye with us?"

"Aye, duke, that I am," replied the engineer, throwing his arms around the surprised duke and thumping him on the back.

Right away it was agreed that Mr. Brindley would stay at the Hall. The duke himself showed Mr. Gilbert and me to the door. As we were saying goodnight, he suddenly let out a howl of rage, disappeared into the house and came back with a cane.

"That damned gardener has been planting flowers again. I won't have such frippery around my hall."

So saying he whacked off the heads of the offending blooms with his cane. I ran to catch up with Mr. Gilbert, who was laughing quietly to himself as he walked down the village lane.

CHAPTER · 9

The Clock Strikes Thirteen

As soon as Mr. Brindley took charge of the canal construction, matters improved rapidly. He was popular with the workmen who, because of his rough ways and homely speech, accepted him as one of their own. When some accident happened he would curse more vigorously than the duke, but in his Derbyshire accent. If there was a difficult problem to be solved, he would retire to his bed until he had the answer.

The sough was now officially called the underground canal and at Mr. Brindley's orders a second arm was constructed parallel to the first. They were to meet half a mile underground; one was for boats going into the mine and one for those leaving it.

His grace had no more pressing concerns than money. Small wonder he never relented in his search for more coal. It was clear, as the duke insisted, that a canal must have coals at the heels of it, and more coal would have to be found, for the profit from his Worsley mine was less than one hundred pounds a year.

So men were sent to delve on Walkden Moor. His grace liked to watch them hammer the long hollow bores into the earth and drag them out to see if any coal was forced up inside them. The men hated to cease work for their midday meal while he was watching. Old David Llewellen finally approached his employer and explained the problem. His grace accepted this and promptly at noon as the work's yard clock struck twelve, he left the men alone. However, one time he and I were passing by at one o'clock and the men were nowhere in sight. They appeared ten minutes after the hour to find the duke waiting, gold watch in hand. He demanded an explanation.

"Well, your grace," said Llewellen, in his musical Welsh speech, " 'tis easy to hear twelve strike, but a man can easily miss the single stroke."

The duke said nothing. He knew two men had watches, one of them, a gift, finer than his own. That very day he sent me to Eccles for John Collier, the clockmaker, and gave him careful instructions.

Three days later, promptly at one o'clock, everyone except his grace was astonished to hear the work's yard clock strike, not once but thirteen times! For days after, wherever the duke went, he wore a look of triumph on his face.

Other economies were forced upon him. It was said that all his clothes were made by Baxter, the miners' tailor. His brown top coat had large gold buttons, one of which was missing, and his brown worsted breeches were of strangely old-fashioned cut; they were fastened at the knee with silver buckles. Nor did he favor a wig, preferring most of the time to tie his hair in a queue. I was present when Aubrey summoned up the courage to tell his master he must dress in accordance with his station in life.

"But Aubrey," replied the duke, "in London no one knows me so it matters not how I dress."

"But here in Worsley, your grace ..."

"It matters less, sithee, for here everyone knows who I am." And that ended the matter.

I had already noticed a distinct coolness between his grace and the Vicar of Eccles. It arose on the vexed matter of the duke's church tithes, which had not been paid for some time. Sunday sermons at St. Mary's Church of late had become more and more devoted to parables on the subject of money. We just sat behind the duke's two pews, and it seemed to us that the vicar looked a great deal in his direction. The duke squirmed considerably, but attempted to put a brave face on it.

After service, his grace was always quick to leave, but one Sunday in October, Mr. Crookhall, the Vicar of Eccles, preached a sermon about the talents of silver. The rector let the vicar finish the service while he lay in ambush for his noble patron. The duke fell into the trap. Desperately trying to ignore him, he took to his heels with the rector in pursuit. It was a fierce contest but finally, exhausted, the duke flung himself into a saw pit, where he had, perforce, to promise to pay his church tithes. Which he did.

The days were now growing shorter and colder; winter was fast approaching. I was sitting with the Pendletons in front of a smoky fire when Mr. Paul, the butcher, called. He had spent the last few nights working his way from house to house killing any surplus animals. I thought it a cruel business much to the surprise of the Pendletons.

"We can't afford to feed all our stock, George," protested Mrs. Pendleton. "There's no extra food for animals in winter."

"Besides," added her daughter, "there's a lot of good food to be eaten after the pigsticker's bin by."

We had three piglets left, and these were killed. The bacon was salted and smoked in a shed belonging to a collier who lived across the common. Black puddings were made from the blood, and lard was available for cakes and puddings. One thing I refused to do was to eat a meal of trotters with the Pendletons. It was as much as I could do to watch the two of them scale the horn covering off the feet.

"You don't know what you're missing, George," said Mrs. Pendleton. "Try one."

But I couldn't. For one thing, I'd fed the pigs every day; I just couldn't bring myself to eat their feet!

It didn't worry Peg. She ate six!

Mr. Brindley, Peg and I traveled everywhere. We had

horses; the engineer was very fond of his mare, Sal. Peg and I could hardly sit our ponies at first, but after spending more time out of the saddle than in, we got the hang of things.

Most of our time was spent surveying the route of the canal and talking with landowners, some of whom were concerned that the canal would scar the landscape and, at my suggestion, the duke, complaining bitterly of the cost, paid an artist six guineas to paint several canvasses of what the countryside would look like once the canal was finished. I thought the paintings very fine, but his grace dismissed them as fripperies.

The construction of the canal fascinated me, but nothing amazed me so much as puddling. Mr. Brindley explained its purpose to us.

"You see, lad," he said. "Up 'til now we've cut through clay, there's bin no problem." He searched for his tobacco pouch and tinderbox. "But this is soil, and it's usually porous; the water seeps through. So we have to line the canal and make it watertight."

He pointed with his pipe stem at three men in a shallow pit. They were pouring sand and water onto clay.

"Them's the men who will make this canal a success or failure."

One of the men sat down and unlaced his boots. Next he rolled up his trousers and stepped into the pit.

"Those men," said Mr. Brindley, "will stamp puddle for ten hours a day."

We watched them add more clay, sand and water.

Soon, all three were in the pit squishing the mixture underfoot.

"But why use their feet?" I asked; "couldn't they mix it with shovels?"

"Nay," replied Mr. Brindley, " 'Tis a question of feel. Puddle has to be just so, and them men can sense it by the way it moves underfoot.

"They has to know just what they're at," he continued, sticking his pipe between his teeth and leading the way back to the horses. "Too thick clay'll crack; too thin won't hold water."

"How thick is the puddle on this canal?" I asked.

"Depends," replied the engineer. "Oft times it be six feet. We'll have three to six feet most of the way I've chosen. 'Tis vital and there's no worse crime than cutting a canal bank. 'Tis far worse than slitting the baize on his grace's billiard table."

Within a week the rain ceased and the first snows began. Day after day flakes fell until there was a carpet three feet deep. Everything lay smothered under a blanket of white. It was the earliest snowfall anyone could remember. Laborers sought in vain for tools left outside. Only the outline of the canal could be seen. Cutters still dug, laborers tried their best to move earth, but their wheelbarrows slid off the planks and toppled them, earth and all, back into the ditch. In places, drifts ten feet high reared above the land. Woods once leafy and green lay stark and bare. Without warning the wind would rise and drive its white army against us. Men literally disappeared from sight for hours on end in blizzards. Two almost died of exposure only ten yards from a house, unable to see a foot before them or to make their cries heard above the howling wind.

All work ceased for three days at the start of November. The duke fretted, but could do nothing. When the worst was over, work began in appalling conditions and continued in worse. Yet no man abandoned his duty; all knew that the duke had staked all on his canal. Each man knew that should the duke fail, he would drag him down with him.

It wasn't all work. On November 5 the duke ordered a celebration on Pope Day. For days the young people of Worsley, including Peg and me, had been collecting dead wood for the bonfire. Quite a few rickety palings had been taken from local fences, and I suspect a few pieces of timber had been cut from the duke's lands.

The bonfire was built on the far side of Worsley Common, where flying sparks presented no danger. It was agreed that no fireworks were to be set off because of the danger of fire, but a "Guy Fawkes" was stuffed with straw and clad in a suit of clothes I had once seen the duke wearing. As the "Guy" was perched on top, Aubrey, the duke's valet, was looking very pleased with himself.

When the bonfire was lit, the duke said to me, "A fine Guy Fawkes, Icarus, and were it not for the dark lantern in its hand and the paper miter on its head, it might be said to resemble a certain duke. You haven't seen Aubrey, have you?"

As the flames reached the effigy, the villagers trooped around the bonfire, many carrying flaming torches and wearing masks. In chorus they shouted:

> *Please to remember the fifth of November*
> *Gunpowder, treason, and plot*
> *We know no reason why gunpowder treason*
> *Should ever be forgot.*

Peg and I walked around the roaring fire with the rest. Already the younger children were putting potatoes into the ashes while their parents prepared mulled ale. I felt a little foolish myself. Somehow, in the excitement, I had taken Peg's hand, and I couldn't think of a reason to let go. I'll say this though, now that she didn't work in the mine, she had become a lot prettier.

It was so cold that a daily fire became essential. Mrs. Pendleton decided the cottage chimney had to be cleaned. The women took the tin bath outside and filled it with water from Worsley Brook. Meanwhile I had to stick my head up the chimney, and with the advice and encouragement of the two of them, poke around with a holly bush until all the soot was dislodged.

"Looks like a real collier now, don't 'e, Ma?" said Peg, as I spluttered outside to clean up in the bath.

In mid-December a second great snowstorm began. Sometimes the snow fell in great swirling heaps; at others drifting flakes fluttered down lazily, adding themselves to the mantle spread across Worsley.

The village looked cleaner than usual, though around chimneys there was the familiar black smoke and the sight of brickwork where the snow had melted. But on the ground, from the Grapes to Worsley Common everything lay below an ocean of white.

Only the dedication of the duke, the determination of his agent and engineer, and the mighty efforts of the laborers kept the work progressing.

Then late in December disaster struck. One bitterly cold night an embankment burst. The watchmen were able to block the hole with a flat boat, but most of the water had drained away.

The next day as soon as it was light we all went to look at the damage.

"Look here," said the engineer, "see these pieces of puddle with holes through them?"

Peg picked up a piece. "Looks like moles," she said.

"In December?" demanded Mr. Brindley. "Them's human moles more like."

He would say nothing more and immediately retired to his bed where he remained the rest of the day.

CHAPTER · 10

A Quarrel

What happened outside the mine had less effect on the underground canal. There six men drove through rock, shale, clay, and sandstone, hammering, hacking, and blasting their way northwards. The two tunnels were joined some eight hundred yards from the entrance. There was a brief celebration when the two teams of cutters met, and the duke made a pretty speech, which few heard because the sound of his voice echoed from all sides. Then his health was drunk in strong ale, and a sign stuck up saying, "Waters Meeting, 1759."

The duke was very anxious to win coal again. Very little had been got while the underground canals were pushed northwards. However, the twin arms of the underground canal had become one, and as the canal progressed northward under Walkden Moor, water that had flooded old workings began to drain into it, for it was well below the level of the old sough.

It was now possible to get coal from the Worsley

four-foot seam to the duke's great relief. Mr. Brindley devised a clever way of getting a large number of boats back into the mine. He was able, by means of something he called a sluice, to make the water flow back into the mine so that boats were always assisted by the current of water in both directions.

"I'll bet ye never thought of putting water into a mine, did ye, duke," he said as he demonstrated the sluice.

"Indeed not," said his grace, studiously avoiding looking at me. "Indeed not."

One day I was in the mine about some business of the duke's when Black Tom called to me from a narrow tunnel.

"George, does tha think ther's owt beautiful in this mine?"

"Doesn't seem likely, Tom."

"Well, follow me and we'll do marvels for tha education."

We crawled downhill some twenty yards and then turned sharply to the right and continued in an upward direction for forty more.

"Now put out tha candle and tak' a look."

Before us was a flooded working, but it was as if the fairy folk had transformed it. In the darkness plants glowed against the inky blackness of the coal. Some of them were long and white, like thick spider webs. Others contrasted with them and looked like tawed leather.

"It's like the fairy kingdom," I gasped.

A sort of silver moss grew on the walls, roof, and pillars of coal. When I looked directly at it, my eyes were dazzled. I could see every detail of Black Tom in the silver light.

"Is this not beauty?" he demanded.

"It is, indeed," I answered in awe. "I never dreamed there could be such things."

"Aye, 'tis a sight an' all. I have been in places where the very rocks themselves glowed all the colors of the rainbow."

I gazed upon the enchanted world until Black Tom struck his flint and lit a mutton-fat candle.

I turned to follow him as he led the way back to the main road. As I did so, my feet caught something that clattered against the rock floor.

Tom came back to see what it was.

"By gar," he said. " 'Tis my old snap tin. I lost it some five years ago when this working was flood out."

He opened it. "Whew!" he said, quickly slamming it shut. " 'Twill need a good scalding before it's much use again. Wouldst tha care for it, George? A souvenir of a visit to fairyland?"

And I have that snap tin to this very day. In it I keep my pens and inks. It is one of my most prized possessions, and when asked about it, I reply that it was a gift from the fairy folk.

Soon the holiday season was upon us. Everyone got three days off and Christmas dinner was the finest meal I ever saw. There were mince pies in the shape of coffins; they were supposed to be the manger at Bethlehem! We drank plum porridge, which was a sort of soup made with raisins and, I suspect, French brandy.

But this was only the beginning. We had killed the goose and cooked him in orange sauce. Then, to cap it all, there was a huge round plum pudding decorated with a sprig of holly. I was admiring it when, to my surprise, Mrs. Pendleton poured a sauce over it and took a candle and touched it to the sauce. There was a bang, a roar, and then the whole pudding burst into flames.

"A brandy sauce, George," she said as the flames died down. "It adds the final touch."

It certainly did. I had two large helpings.

I was glad to join the carol singers. It gave me a chance to shake the dinner down. Some twenty of us, bearing two lanterns on long poles, walked around the common singing Christmas carols. Peg said she felt cold and had to stay close to me for warmth. That was rather strange because it was, for once, quite a warm night, and she wore a heavy cloak.

The day after Christmas was Boxing Day, and all the village was about early taking Christmas presents to their friends and sharing in the pleasure and gratitude of those who received them.

His grace sent me a very fine penknife with which I could cut quill pens for casting up his accounts. He gave Peg a very silly hat with plumes and ribbons. She wore it all day and quite flattened her curls.

Mrs. Pendleton was presented with a fine cheese sent from Devonshire. It was called Blue Vinney and was so ripe that it crumbled to the touch.

In return, we worked a morning for the duke cutting ice from his ponds and canal. We covered the blocks of ice with salt and wrapped them in flannel strips before storing them in an ice house. He wanted to make something called ice cream, but none of us would use ice from the canal despite the duke's insistence that the water was pure and had health-giving properties.

Thus the Christmas season was a joyful one for me, for I had found new friends, a home, and work. No doubt, in good time all would, as the duke said, be revealed. There was a great deal to thank God for, and I had done so at the Christmas Eve thanksgiving service at St. Mary's.

And so December passed, and we celebrated the new year, 1760, praying at a special midnight ceremony for a happy and prosperous year. It was a double ceremony for us, for Peg's fifteenth birthday was December 31. We toasted her health in ale and gave her a fine linen shawl.

No sooner had we celebrated these events than we were feasting again on Twelfth Night. The entire village seemed to be crammed into the Grapes. The duke's health was drunk a dozen times and, not surprisingly, he got the bill.

Not long after this a dispute arose between, of all people, Mr. Gilbert and Mr. Brindley. The engineer, something of a crusty bachelor, lavished much affection on his mare, Sal. One night someone let Sal into the field where Mr. Gilbert's horse, a roan stallion of fiery mettle, was tethered. In the morning the two animals were discovered together, and it took no skill in horses to know that in eleven months Sal would bear a foal. Mr. Brindley was furious and sent a note by me to Mr. Gilbert. I saw a copy of it later.

> *Sir* [it began,] *I send this meshender to you to tell you that your stalion has got my sal in foal. This was no prakitikal jok; but the act of a blagard, yes, a blagard. You did it to prevent me from doing my work properly. So, Sir, henceforth let us have no more sosiety.*
>
> Yor honble servunt,
Brindley

The recipient of this note professed ignorance of the whole matter. He and his son Tom rode over to the Hall to see the sulky engineer.

I heard later from Aubrey that there was a lot of shouting from the testy engineer and much quiet, persuasive talk from the Gilberts. Anyway, Aubrey said, they emerged later arm in arm and strolled to the Grapes where they drank a great deal of very strong ale long into the night.

Now I'm not one to inform on others so I kept my own counsel. What I do know is that on the night the two animals got acquainted, it was a certain young lady's turn to stable our ponies. When she got home, she had a very strange air about her and chuckled at my reading from *Pilgrim's Progress,* even during some of the most moving passages.

CHAPTER · 11

The Old Navigators

As the surface canal moved west, the fleet of boats moved with it. Flat rafts were loaded down with tools belonging to blacksmiths, carpenters, cutters, laborers, and masons. Rocks and soil dug and blasted from the diggings were brought in ballast boats and used to build up embankments in low-lying areas. It was steady progress, especially as men had to labor in snow and ice, sometimes chest deep in icy water.

The duke began serving mulled ale on the coldest days. The servers heated irons until they glowed red, then plunged them into pewter tankards of ale. Peg and I were allowed a pint each day, the cutters got four.

There was a brief respite during February on St. Valentines's Day. Mr. Gilbert told me what I should do, for I had never heard of it.

"Usually," he said, "a young man sends his Valentine a present, but now there are Valentine cards."

I bought a Valentine card while in Leigh about the duke's business. It had two hearts fashioned from red silk with an arrow through them. Cupid flew across one corner holding his bow and arrow. Inside was written "Love is but a madrigal." I signed it with an "X."

I didn't think I would get a card, but I did. It was addressed to George; the "r" was backwards.

As for Margaret Pendleton, she received six! They were all pushed under the door late at night. She was unbearably smug all week.

A mile from the River Irwell Mr. Brindley nailed up a board to show the level of the canal at that point. It soon became known as "Duke's Folly," for few outside Worsley thought the canal would ever reach that point, and if it did, it was confidently predicted that the Third Duke of Bridgewater would be a pauper and unable to afford the expensive flight of locks necessary to lower his boats into the Irwell.

One evening, soon after Valentine's Day, a cold gray night, when Peg and her mother and I were all drawn close to the fire, there was an urgent knock at the door. There stood Aubrey.

"T'lad mun go to the Hall at once," he said, "at once mind."

I hurried away pulling my outer coat as I went. Aubrey stayed at the cottage warming himself by the fire.

At the Hall, Mr. Brindley himself admitted me.

"In the library, the duke's in a *real* pother."

The room was a shambles. Books were scattered left and right, maps and drawings lay across every flat surface. The floor was covered with chalk marks.

The duke was kneeling on the floor surveying a long column of figures which totaled £238,000.

" 'Tis no use, John," he was saying as we entered, "I'm ruined."

No one paid any attention to me as I sat and waited; I knew it was serious for not one pipe was lit. Finally the duke looked up.

"I thought you should know," he said, "for you've labored mightily in your way. The canal's a lost cause. A total loss. Ten thousand pounds sunk in a hole in the ground."

"Nay, duke," said Brindley, " 'tis not the end of the world. Be of good cheer."

"Aye, aye, Brindley, but what's to be done?"

"Perhaps," I suggested, "you could tell me what's happened."

Mr. Gilbert took up a sheet of paper while the duke helped himself to the decanter of port.

"Well, George" said the agent. "As you know, we planned to take the canal to the Irwell, and then use that navigation to carry our boats to Manchester."

I nodded.

"Lord Strange and the other owners of the Irwell Navigation refuse to accept our barges at anything less than the full toll of twelve shillings a ton—twice the cost of the coal itself, three shillings more than agreed upon."

"That means," added Mr. Brindley, "that the duke's coal will cost more than any other. No one's going to pay tuppence a hundredweight more for coal than he has to."

"It's worse than that," said the duke, rising and draining his glass. "Once news of this gets out, no one will advance me money to finish a canal to nowhere."

I dug among the papers until I found the map of the canal route.

"I might have guessed this of Strange," continued the duke. "The fellow waited until I was powerless to change direction. O Greek Synon, was there ever such treachery?" He poured himself another glass. "Even his title is assumed. He's only a Stanley, and they have no rights to the barony of Strange. Well, drink up all of ye, for there'll be little more of this to come."

An idea was slowly forming in my mind—a wild, fantastic idea so mad that I had to force myself to speak.

"If I were your grace," I ventured, "I would carry the canal on a bridge over the River Irwell and—"

"Over the Irwell," gasped the duke, "by heavens, John, the lad's taken boggarts."

Even Mr. Gilbert was smiling as he said, "A castle in the air, eh George?"

"But look at the map," I replied. "If the canal were built in a stone or clay trough, well puddled, of course, and crossed above the Irwell, it could turn east to Manchester and west to Liverpool."

"Madness," said the Duke of Bridgewater.

Mr. Brindley said nothing.

"I shall listen to no more nonsense this night," said the duke. "Already people speak of the Duke's Folly. Am I now to be ridiculed for building castles in the air? A good night to ye all." And with that, taking the decanter of port, he left the room.

I prepared to go, but Mr. Gilbert said, "Stay, George, it may be a long night, for I know what Brindley's thinking, and his thoughts are not unlike my own, I warrant."

There was no sleep for any of us that night. Mr. Gilbert sent Aubrey, who had just returned, back to Mrs. Pendleton's to tell her not to worry and then on to his wife to tell her he would be staying at the Hall for the night.

Meanwhile, Mr. Brindley lit his pipe and began sketching on the floor. When he had a sketch he liked, Mr. Gilbert made a beautiful plan of it on paper.

They had frequent arguments and once Mr. Brindley referred to his horse's predicament, but by six in the morning the drawings were done and the windows opened to let in the morning air.

I had spent most of my time bringing in steaming dishes of coffee and picking up after the men. When Mr. Brindley said I could scrub the floor and replace the carpet, I knew that a decision had been made.

None of us went to bed. It didn't seem worth it. We were at breakfast when the duke came down in his morning gown. After he learned that we had been there all night, had finished four bottles of wine and drunk most of his coffee, he groaned loudly. And when Mr. Gilbert told him that it *was* possible to take the canal over the river Irwell, he all but collapsed.

Mr. Brindley handed the duke several drawings to

study. He inspected them carefully before laying them down and saying, "Well, Brindley, I believe you might be right, so you and Gilbert just finish the work in your own way. I'll get the brass somehow."

Word spread through Worsley that the duke had a new scheme afoot—a plan so daring that men would judge him a lunatic. Gradually, as the details were known, villagers huddled in groups and shook their heads in wonder. Surely the duke, his engineer, and his agent could not all be mad?

Visitors from beyond Worsley openly mocked the duke's scheme. A pamphlet war was fought between the duke's party and those like the Byroms, Brookes, and Mrs. Chetham who favored the cause of the Old Navigators and their leader, Lord Strange. We, for our part, pointed out that Lord Strange and the other proprietors had done nothing to improve their waterway despite extortionate tolls and high-handed manners.

The Old Navigators claimed that the new canal would ruin them, and when that gained them little sympathy, they accused the duke of borrowing money for a plan that would inevitably result in a financial loss greater than that of the South Sea Bubble. But when it became clear that he was determined to go ahead and build his "castle in the air," they called a public meeting to urge the signing of a petition against him.

His grace summoned me to the Hall. "George, I want you and Gilbert at that meeting. Have some figures ready just in case. I can't go myself for fear of appearing on the defensive. Gilbert will speak on my behalf if necessary. I tell thee, the opening battles of this war will be fought in committee rooms and not under Walkden Moor."

And so three days later the duke bought me a new fine woolen coat of pale gold with silk knee britches of the same shade. The waistcoat was of the new shorter style, which showed the breeches underneath. They were fastened at the knee by silver buckles. I looked like the son of some great lord and flattered myself that I might well be.

"You must powder this night, George," said the duke, "but, as Mrs. Pendleton has no powder closet, pray do it outside her cottage door."

The duke surveyed me critically before Mr. Gilbert and I left for Warrington Town Hall. He pronounced himself satisfied.

"The expense is justified," he declared. "We must not give the impression I lack for money."

It was a cool night but not unpleasant. Mr. Gilbert was quiet, and I did not intrude upon his thoughts.

"This is a risky business, this aqueduct," he said suddenly. "Very risky. Should it fail, his grace will lose everything. He could survive that, but he could not bear to see his dream destroyed."

"Do you believe it will succeed?" I asked, flicking my pony's reins to keep pace with him.

"In all honesty, I cannot be certain. Brindley is confident, but no Englishman has ever built an aqueduct.

And should it miscarry, the whole of Worsley will fall on evil days. His grace knows that. He is a strange mixture of idealism and practicality."

An hour later we were in Warrington Town Hall. I had prepared some lists of figures in case they were called for, but Mr. Gilbert was sure the meeting would be too stormy for such matters, and so it proved to be. The Old Navigators were in their own country, and those who worked at the many enterprises linked to their navigation muttered threateningly when we entered. To my relief, however, there was a resounding cheer from a large group of brawny miners sitting in the back of the room.

Mr. Gilbert smiled. "I wasn't going to walk into the lions' den without a few friends," he whispered.

Lord Strange was apparently to be chairman of the meeting.

"Score one for them," said Mr. Gilbert when he saw this.

It was my first contact with Lord Strange, the man who was to cause me so much pain later. He was heavyset, above medium height, with burning eyes that retreated deep behind thick, bushy eyebrows. The white line of a scar traced its path across his left cheek. His lips were thin, and he had a habit of biting on the lower one.

He wore a white cambric shirt adorned with small ruffles and a stock of the same material. A deep blue frock coat with silver buttons was cut away to reveal a white silk waistocat, breeches, and stockings. He carried a black cane with a silver wolf's head top which he banged on the table for order.

Lord Strange spoke at length, painting a dark picture of the future if the duke's canal received Parliamentary support. "Ruin stares us in the face," was his theme.

As he finished, there was a loud roar of support, mingled with some solid boos and jeers. Then a cry went up from the supporters of the Old Navigators. "The petition, let us sign the petition."

"A moment, my friends," shouted the duke's agent, striding on to the platform at the front of the hall. He raised his hands for silence. It was several minutes before he could be heard.

"Before you sign the petition let me remind you who supports it. They are the very people who when they had us at their mercy showed us no consideration."

There were cheers at this and a few boos from the front rows. A scuffle or two broke out between miners and boatmen. Lord Strange was scowling.

"But," the agent continued when order was restored, "now they are threatened; they weep crocodile tears and plead injured innocence."

Lord Strange looked as though he would explode. A vein throbbed on his forehead, and he banged on the table with his cane.

"Will you sit, sir?" he shouted, gnawing on his lip.

"I will, my lord," replied Mr. Gilbert, "when I have had my say."

More applause greeted this; there was little booing.

"The Irwell Navigation charges high fees yet is unwilling to carry out the most necessary repairs and maintenance."

"Aye, true, true."

"And they delay, delay, delay, on the pretext of waiting for a flash while produce spoils and deliveries are lost."

At this there was loud applause.

"They promised to build a cut from the Irwell to the Worsley mines. Where is that cut?"

The applause grew louder.

"All his grace is trying to do is find a way to carry coal to Manchester and Salford and improve trade with Liverpool. His goal is to keep prices down."

"Fine enough talk," shouted a fat man with florid face and a tattered peruke. "But I'm a miller, and I can't grind corn without water."

"The Bridgewater Canal will take no water from the Irwell. None at all. We will take our supply from three reservoirs on Walkden Moor. Of course," he added, "if the aqueduct collapses, we will add some water to the Irwell."

This was greeted with shouts of laughter.

"My friends," he concluded, "has his grace or any of his family ever lied or cheated any man here?"

There was silence; then cries of "Never! Never!"

"Have there ever been mysterious accidents late at night to your property?"

There were renewed cries of "Never, never" and a few of "Shame! Shame!"

"Then," continued Mr. Gilbert, "look at the record of the Irwell Navigation. They charge twelve shillings a ton to carry coal from Manchester to Liverpool. When water is low and they cannot get a flash they send goods by road at thirty-five shillings a ton."

There were loud mutters of "Aye! Aye!"

"His grace will charge only six shillings a ton. I have his word on it, and his word is good enough for me."

He walked quickly back to where I stood. The applause was deafening. The miller turned to face the crowd waving his arms for silence.

"We came here to sign a petition, and sign one we shall, but in favor of the Bridgewater Canal. I know many of ye think as I do."

Indeed they did. It seemed that every man in the room wanted to set his mark to the petition. Others pressed around Mr. Gilbert to congratulate him.

Lord Strange and half a dozen of his staunchest supporters pushed their way through the crowd.

"Well, sir, I trust you are happy with this night's work," he said. "Men like you will be the ruin of England. Of all England, sir."

"Do not give me all the credit, my lord," replied Mr. Gilbert. "The idea of the aqueduct was this lad's plan not mine. When water flows over the Irwell, men will praise George here, not me."

At this, there was a roar of applause and laughter from those standing nearby.

"Will they indeed," said Lord Strange, looking at me and tapping his stick into his palm. "Well, I shall not forget him, be assured of that." And glaring darkly at me, he hurried from the room just as a group of miners hoisted Mr. Gilbert and me onto their shoulders and paraded us about the room.

It was a happy, singing band of miners that straggled into the Grapes that night, bearing a petition of one hundred seventeen signatures and marks supporting the duke's new endeavor.

His grace was so delighted with the evening's triumph that he paid for all the drinks without a murmur. Well, *scarcely* a murmur.

II

A Hanging
at Tyburn

CHAPTER · 1 2

The London Coach

I was to go to London; Peg was not. I heard about that, I can tell you! Mr. Brindley had already left on Sal since he intended to spend a day in Glossop about some business of his own. His grace left the same day by post chaise. Peg and I saw him off.

The chaise had room for two inside, and in the dickey behind there was space for Aubrey and some luggage. The postboy (a man of about sixty!) rode on one of the horses. Accompanying the duke was his cousin Samuel Egerton, who wished to visit his London relatives. I heard the duke grumble mightily to Mr. Egerton about the cost, but he took care to be sure that the postboy couldn't hear.

"I gave up my carriage to save money, cut my expenses to four hundred per annum, and now I have to hire a chaise at eighteen pence a mile and pay sixpence every time an ostler changes the horses."

Mr. Gilbert helped Mr. Egerton into the chaise. He

tried to look solemn. "And don't forget, your grace, these fellows expect a tip of threepence a mile."

"Highway robbery," said the duke with a snort, as he settled in, "and this kind is legal."

The reason for all the excitement was that Lord Strange, frustrated by the failure of his petition drive, had devised a new strategy. Realizing that the proposed aqueduct at Barton would need a new act of Parliament, he had left for London where, with the support of powerful friends, including the Earl of Derby, he intended to raise an opposition to the new act.

I was too excited to sleep. Mrs. Pendleton helped me to pack, her daughter merely glared. It was decided I should wear the clothes I had with me when I first arrived in Worsley and an old coat Aubrey found somewhere. A second suit was also packed, and a new frock coat and a three-corner hat with ostrich feathers were added to my wardrobe.

A hired wagon took us to Manchester through a cold, gloomy night with no stars or moon. It was a relief to reach the Swan Inn and warm ourselves by a blazing coal fire.

Promptly at four o'clock the coach arrived. "Mark that, George," said Mr. Gilbert, "that is the last time we will be on time."

It was a magnificent sight. The great heavy coach was covered with dull black leather studded with nails. The frames and the windows were picked out in red, and the windows were covered with leather curtains. The roof was rounded with an outside seat at the back over the boot where our luggage was stowed and chained down.

The four horses were covered with cloths, but these were being removed by a groom as he backed the animals between the shafts.

"This is the moment of 'putting to'," said Mr. Gilbert. "See how their manes and tails have been plaited."

The animals were anxious to be off; they snorted white smoke in the crisp morning air.

Then the coachman appeared. He was buttoned up to the throat in an enormous box coat of deep green. Immense silver buttons held it tight over his large girth. A white handkerchief was tied about his neck, and on his head was a great tricorne hat with three large black feathers.

"Do you see?" whispered Mr. Gilbert. "The coachman has had his front teeth filed down so he can grasp the whipcords; it is a common practice."

"Can I sit on top with him?"

" 'Twould cost a guinea extra and within four or five miles you'd be begging to travel inside. Besides, I think we will have a guard up this trip."

"I should like to drive that team," I said wistfully. "Just see how they stamp their feet and look at the glossy sheen of their coats."

The guard was not so striking as the driver. He wore corduroy breeches and dull leather boots. His topcoat might once have been white. The brim of his hat was so big that it hid the crown. A rosette, whose colors had blended into each other, was stuck on the left brim. He bore a blunderbuss under one arm and carried a horn in his right. Laboriously, he hauled himself alongside the driver. The whole coach swayed.

We hurried inside; there were no other passengers. The guard blew a loud blast on his horn, and with a clatter of hooves on cobblestones and much creaking of the wooden coach, we were off.

"Most people try to sleep at first," said Mr. Gilbert. "After a while the roads become so bad and the stops for tolls so frequent that little rest is possible."

I may have dozed a little, but sleep was difficult. At every bump, the coach jolted and the noise of the iron-banded wheels almost deafened me.

Before five miles passed, we were sitting in the corners hanging onto leather straps.

At Stockport we picked up two more passengers, a farmer named Ezra Gentry and an excessively fat woman who talked only of food. She took up half the room in the coach.

Farmer Gentry sat on the opposite side to me. "It is a chilly morning," he said, closing the curtain near him, "and 'twill likely snow within the hour. Pox on't; I've two hundred ewes lambing. One good wind and every lambing pen will be down." He pulled his greatcoat tightly around his thin body, thrust his hands into his pockets, and promptly fell asleep.

"If it does," said the woman, reaching into a bag she carried and selecting a large red apple, "I'll be late for supper."

With this gloomy prospect in view, she lapsed into silence, breaking it regularly with large bites of her apple.

The farmer was wrong. Dawn revealed low-lying clouds that soon started dropping torrents of rain. Even the leather curtains couldn't keep us dry. Roads that had been bad before now became rivers of mud. The men had to dismount at each hill and walk alongside the coach; often we pushed when the going got too much for the horses.

"The worst thing about rain is that it fills the ruts and the kids float away," said Mr. Gilbert.

" 'Tis all too true," agreed Farmer Gentry, "and they never get replaced."

"Kids?" I asked.

"Aye, lad," said the farmer, kicking a small pile of brushwood that lay before him. "That's a kid. The owners of the turnpike sometimes place them in ruts to make the ride smoother. They never last more'n a week at best."

I actually saw holes four feet deep floating with mud, and we passed one abandoned coach with broken axles.

By afternoon the rain seemed to have spent its force.

"I think the weather is improving," said Mr. Gilbert. "I see brighter skies to the south."

"True, true," said the farmer somewhat reluctantly, "but soon we shall leave the turnpike for many miles of mill road."

The driver called us back in, and from the boot he pulled out a pile of straw which he spread inside the coach.

" 'Twill help keep the chill out," he said.

"So they say," grumbled the farmer, "but 'tis fear of the mud on our coats and boots that concerns him."

The road improved once we got to Buxton. We stopped at the Eagle and Child to warm ourselves and clean off the mud while the landlord bustled around serving mulled ale to those who wanted it. I got hot chocolate.

By noon that day we were feeling better. Our female companion left us ten miles beyond Buxton, so there was more room inside, and even Gentry admitted that more rain was unlikely.

We might have made fairly good time, but every five miles we had to stop and pay tolls. Nevertheless we were almost at Derby when disaster struck. It was early evening, and we were walking behind when the guard let out a shout, "Mad dog." We all scrambled back into the coach as the guard discharged his blunderbuss, frightening the dog but missing it by a mile. The excitement upset the horses, and the off-leader shied and entangled himself in the reins. At this the remaining horses took fright and bolted.

The coachman did what he could, but hauling on the reins was not enough. Up the hill we went, all shouting "whoa" until at the top the coach struck a "take-off" stone and toppled on its side.

I fell to the floor, the other two fell on me. We were collecting our wits when the door above us opened and the anxious face of the driver peered in.

"Anyone hurt?"

"Probably" was the farmer's reply, but apart from my face, which he used as a stepping-stone, there appeared to be no great harm done.

The horses were in a dreadful state, so tangled up that we had to cut the reins to free them. The coachman and Farmer Gentry managed to calm them. The bay mare was lame in the near foreleg, and the farmer led her to a nearby stream to keep the swelling down. He wanted to bleed her in the neck, but I made such a fuss that it wasn't done.

Mr. Gentry, who knew the countryside, volunteered to ride for help, and one of the horses was gentled down for his use. He rode off, warning us not to expect help before nightfall.

It was only an hour, however, before he reappeared. An ostler and two fresh horses accompanied him.

Ropes were secured around the coach and fastened to the horses. Then, with loud cracking of whips, shouting, and a few oaths from coachman and ostler, the coach was righted. A close inspection revealed several broken spokes in the front wheel, but the axles had held.

And so, carrying all but the heaviest luggage, we straggled along the road for five miles until we saw the welcome sight of the Angel Inn.

Our host hastened up the road to greet us. Seizing my burden, he led us through the archway into the spacious inn yard.

"Welcome, welcome," he said. "Welcome to the Angel Inn."

He had a bright red scarf knotted above his bushy wig. A white ruffled shirt was almost hidden by a long blue and white striped apron. His wife also hurried out to greet us. By his side she looked thinner than a pick handle, and her lace cap gave her a rather comic appearance.

"Welcome, welcome," she said. "Supper will be served in twenty minutes."

"Nelly, show Farmer Gentry to the Paragon Room. Duke of Bridgewater's party, follow me to the Crescent."

He hustled us across the reception hall and up the main staircase. The walls were all panelled and the furniture was made from a black wood.

"In here, gentlemen," he said, opening an extensive bedroom. "No need to share beds tonight; there are plenty to spare."

The huge four poster beds were large and curtained, with several mattresses plump with feathers. Climbing the short ladder, I flung myself, mud and all, onto the bed. Above me was a huge canopy supported by four wooden posts.

"Mahogany," said Mr. Gilbert, tapping one with his knuckles. "It is hard and will take a brilliant polish."

There was a knock at the door and the ostler and a lad brought in our luggage and a basin of hot water. Mr. Gilbert tipped the ostler threepence which pleased him mightily.

"It always pays to present servants with excessive vails, George. Many a visitor to an inn has regretted his miserliness," he said. "While I am shaving, you may care to examine the windows closely. I think they will amuse you."

I rolled off my four feather mattresses, mystified by what he had said. Examining the glass window panes, I discovered that almost all of them were covered with signatures and little verses.

"How is it done?" I asked.

"Perhaps a better question is why is it done?" he said, carefully shaving around his chin. He wiped his razor clean on the towel and joined me at the window. "Usually a ring is used. Anything with a diamond will cut glass. Some people have diamond pencils especially made for inscribing windows."

We entered the coffee room some ten minutes later. I had washed the worst stains of the journey from my face and hands and changed into a fresh coat and breeches. Our companion, Farmer Gentry, was already seated at the head of a long table positively groaning under the weight of the food piled on it.

All around on shelves were pewter dishes and plates. At the far end was the kitchen. Strings of onions and garlic hung from the rafters. Our hostess, now dressed in a white apron, was basting a haunch of beef with a large wooden spoon. It was on a spit in front of the fire. What amazed me was that the spit was turned by a small dog suspended in a cage a foot below the ceiling. The little black terrier, whose name was Beulah, ran on a treadmill connected by a pulley and rope to the turnspit. As the dog ran merrily along in her cage, the joint of beef turned slowly and was evenly cooked on all sides.

"If only Brindley could see that," said Mr. Gilbert, "he would find a use for Beulah in Worsley."

From the ovens came the delicious smell of fresh baked bread and honey sauce. Other guests joined us at the table, and I took a glass or two of wine and became quite a spritely conversationalist. The wine seemed to help.

"Eat! Eat!" was all our host ever said, and we gave a good account of ourselves. There was salmon served with fennel sauce, melted butter, and lemon pickle. A neck of pork roasted with gooseberries and a pigeon pie followed. My two-prong fork and flat knife were never stilled, though I had more and more trouble balancing peas on my knife.

The host pressed upon me a wine called Lisbon. It was thick and heavy, and I tasted blackberries and boiled turnip in it. For well over an hour the room was filled with gnawing and sucking on the bones of birds and rinsing of mouths from water bowls.

When I felt I should burst, the cloth was removed, and in came our host and his wife bearing gooseberry and currant tarts and a strange fruit called a melon. Wine and cider and several cheeses with biscuits were also served. Mr. Gilbert made a fine speech in which he called all the ladies present "pretty flowers." At this all of them pretended to be embarrassed.

The ladies retired after the first toast, but the men continued to drink from the port decanter. I had a few glasses myself, assuring Mr. Gilbert, who looked somewhat anxious, that I had never felt better in my life.

Several stories were told as the port decanter circled the company. When it was Mr. Gilbert's turn, he turned to me and said, "I don't think you have heard this tale, George, and it bears retelling."

It seems that just as I was blundering through the woods above the Delph, the Duke of Bridgewater and his agent were conferring by the side of the old sough. His grace paused during his discourse to refresh himself from his snuff box. He inhaled mightily as usual and let out a thundercrack of a sneeze.

Less than a second later, I fell from the top of the sandstone cliff and entered the basin with such force that water doused his grace and Mr. Gilbert.

"Damme," roared the duke, "did you mark that, John? I've slain an eagle with a sneeze. Fish it out, for none will believe it without the bird to show."

Everyone thought this the funniest story yet. I grinned somewhat foolishly, but was pleased to be the center of things and joined in the hearty laughter. Soon after I felt very sleepy. The room was too hot and the smoke was hurting my eyes. Mr. Gilbert had to help me from the room; there were many anxious inquiries after my health, but I waved cheerily to show that all was well. The agent began a lecture on something or other as he helped me undress, but whatever it was, I remembered naught of it.

CHAPTER · 13

The High Toby

We rose at four o'clock the next morning. I had some difficulty; my head was aching and my throat was dry. Mr. Gilbert suggested I stick my head under the pump outside in the inn yard. After doing so, I felt much better.

Breakfast was a slight meal compared with the feast of the night before and in less than half an hour we were boarding the Bath coach to Kenilworth.

The new driver was a thin shifty-looking fellow and the guard so immensely fat that he did not venture down from the box for fear he could not clamber back.

This coach was little different from the one that had brought us to Derby. It was covered with the usual broadheaded nails. There were oval windows in the quarters, and the frame was painted red. Coachman and guard sat up front upon a narrow boot. Behind was an immense basket supported by iron bars that held the luggage. Chalked all over the coach was "No Popery."

There was a blast from the horns, and the coach,

creaking and groaning, rattled under the archway and headed south for Lichfield.

"Doesn't look like rain," observed Mr. Gilbert, settling into a corner.

"True, true," said Farmer Gentry, who sat opposite him, "but all that rain yesterday will have turned the road to mud, and this is a very dangerous stretch. 'Tis infested with highwaymen. You'll soon see a few gentlemen of the road, I'll warrant ye."

I did not understand this remark until we left Buxton. As we rounded a curve in the road, I saw three gibbets by the roadside. From the crossbeam, dangling horribly in chains, hung the remains of three men.

" 'Tis a sight you must get used to," remarked the farmer, drawing a flask of eau-de-vie from one of his greatcoat pockets and offering it to Mr. Gilbert, who hastily declined. "These 'collectors,' as they call themselves, think it fine sport to rob passengers of their excess wealth. I never carry my watch in a coach."

Since Mr. Gilbert had refused his flask, he passed it up through the window to the driver and guard. It was gone a considerable time before it returned. Soon thereafter we heard some lusty off-key blasts on the guard's horn.

"I've heard of Dick Turpin," said Mr. Gilbert.

"I met that gentleman some twenty odd years ago," said the farmer looking sorrowfully at his empty flask. "A pretty rogue he was. Took a watch from me, a purse from my first wife, and said we could have them back if my wife would give him a kiss. 'Twas five years before she would enter a coach after that."

"I hope we don't meet him," I said.

"I hope so too," said the farmer, "for I had the pleasure of seeing him hanged at York in '39."

"I heard something of that from my brother Tom," added Mr. Gilbert. "They say a resurrection was attempted."

"A resurrection?" I asked.

"Aye, lad," said the farmer, drawing his greatcoat around his knees. "There's some who have survived a hanging. The rope doesn't generally break the neck, so a man strangles slow like." He sat back smiling with satisfaction. "When the body is cut down, 'tis not unknown for a surgeon to bring back life into what seemed to be dead. But most men want a quick death and they kicks off their boots so someone will come forward and pull on their legs and make the neck break clean. More merciful, you see. When Dick kept his boots on, all knew what was up."

"Well, what happened?"

"Why the hangman was no fool. By law Dick's clothes and boots were his, so he let the rogue swing for two hours by my new watch. No one bothered to attempt a resuscitation after that."

"I read his goodnight in the *Manchester Mercury*,"said Mr. Gilbert.

"That's a farewell poem from the scaffold, young sir," explained the farmer. "Most of them written well before the turning-off, I might add. 'Tis expected of all highway-men. They confess their sins and beg forgiveness.

"This will be Lichfield," continued the farmer, "I must take my leave, for I expect my farm will have been much neglected during my absence."

We said farewell to him as he boarded a wagon driven by a young woman and rumbled off down the road.

The inn was called the Pair of Compasses. It felt good to stretch our weary limbs. A glass of chocolate put some warmth in our bodies, though Mr. Gilbert needed the additional attention of two glasses of wine.

A new passenger dressed in a black preacher's robe entered the coach with us. His name was Septimus Holker. A black stock, which pushed his cheeks and chin forward, surrounded his neck. The preacher's face was very pale, with eyes too small and buried deep under a pro-truding forehead. His eyebrows were bushy and seemed to bristle every time he spoke, and he nodded approvingly at the "No Popery" signs chalked on the coach.

We had gone less than two miles when a diligence caught us and transferred its passenger. Though not as somberly dressed as Mr. Holker, our new companion was scarcely fashionable. He wore a suit of the same brown color that the Duke of Bridgewater favored. The wrinkled face was surmounted by a bushy bob wig that shed pow-der whenever he moved. At least two metal buttons were missing from his coat and a silver buckle on his black leather shoes was unlatched. A thick cudgel had been thrust in his belt. There was considerable upheaval as he seated himself opposite Mr. Gilbert and me.

"Good day to ye all," he rumbled, "Sam Johnson, London."

The preacher edged away from the newcomer as he settled his bulk in the seat.

Not much was said for a while. Mr. Johnson was constantly twitching or shaking. He was fond of muttering "Tu-tu, tu-tu." His lips were thick, the eyes shortsighted. He seemed to have dropsy, and there were pits on his face as if he had had the smallpox. He contented himself with counting the milestones as we passed them. As we approached Sutton he said, to no one in particular, "English milestones give me much pleasure. They seem to ease me of half the distance of a journey merely by telling me how far I have already gone."

There was another silence while we thought about that. Finally Mr. Gilbert, seeking to break the monotony of the journey, asked him what business he was in.

"I am a writer, sir," he replied. "I have been to visit my brother's and mother's graves to pay my respects. I must now return to London. One of my students has become an actor of note, no doubt his name is known to you—David Garrick."

"Indeed it is, sir," replied Mr. Gilbert, "though I never saw him play."

"He is to appear in *Richard III* shortly, and I have promised to attend."

"And so shall I," promised Mr. Gilbert, "and I shall

take George and encourage my employer, His Grace, the Duke of Bridgewater, to do so."

The preacher had been showing signs of extreme agitation throughout this exchange. Finally he said, "I consider plays the work of the devil. I am horrified that two gentlemen, for so I take you to be, should countenance such fearful goings on. And to speak of them in front of this young—"

"Surely there can be nothing wrong with plays," I said, interrupting him.

"My dear young man," said the preacher earnestly, "I beg of you, on peril of your immortal soul, shun the playhouse as you would the devil himself."

"Sir," said Mr. Johnson, "though I respect the cloth you wear, you are nevertheless talking nonsense. I can only say that David has done much to remove the evils that have surrounded players and playhouses. I also observe from your speech that you are a Scotsman."

"Septimus Holker, Sir, secretary of the Society for the Reformation of Manners. I come from Arbroath, Scotland."

"Well, then," said Mr. Johnson, as if that explained everything.

"I have come to London, the den of iniquity, to save as many as I can in that wicked city."

"Wicked city!" replied Mr. Johnson warmly. "Sir, it is plain you have never been to London. 'Tis the finest habitation in the world. The man who is tired of London is tired of life, for there is everything in

London that a man could desire."

There was little conversation after that. The parson withdrew into his corner, Mr. Johnson to his. We slumbered a little. The stops for tolls were now so common that we were scarce disturbed by them.

We lunched at the Crown and Anchor in Coleshill, on a leg of lamb with parsley sauce. Mr. Johnson, confiding to Mr. Gilbert that he seldom took spirits, loudly ordered two glasses of Geneva in order to irritate Mr. Holker.

At Mr. Gilbert's suggestion, the shutters of the coach were closed, and in the darkness we all dozed fitfully. It was well into evening, just when all were thinking of supper, that the coach halted so suddenly that we were all tumbled to the floor. Mr. Johnson let out an oath as his bob wig flew into Mr. Gilbert's face.

There was a tap on the wooden shutters, and Mr. Gilbert opened them. Outside there was enough light to see the long barrel of a pistol.

The door was opened, and there, in the shadows, sat a highwayman on a large black horse. His pistol was cocked. A thick scarf covered his face and muffled his voice so that we had to strain to hear.

"Please to descend from the coach," he said in a deep voice, sweeping his black tricorne hat from his head in salute.

The parson was first out. "I'll warrant you have little about you," said the highwayman with a laugh.

"Stay here, George," whispered Mr. Gilbert, as he followed Mr. Johnson out.

"You, too, young sir," ordered the horseman, waving his pistol in my direction.

"He's just a lad," said Mr. Gilbert, "he has no money."

"I'll greet him nonetheless, with your permission. Now, sir, descend."

I did as ordered. The highwayman seemed to start; he inspected me closely.

"Your name?"

"George, sir."

"George what—if I may be so bold?"

"George Found, sir."

"I see." He broke off. "Mr. Guard, if you edge one inch nearer that blunderbuss, 'twill be your quietus." He turned back to me.

"And who are these gentlemen, George?"

I looked at Mr. Gilbert, who nodded.

"Mr. Gilbert, agent of the Duke of Bridgewater. This is Mr. Holker, a preacher as you see by his robe. Mr. Johnson is a writer."

"Indeed."

The highwayman turned to Mr. Holker. "And what, reverend sir, is your purpose in making so hazardous a journey?"

"To save the inhabitants of London, that great boil on the skin of England, from the eternal fires of damnation."

"The man's a Scotsman and therefore a fool," said Mr. Johnson. "For there is everything in London that a man could . . ."

"Yes, yes, no doubt," interrupted our captor, "but we are not here to debate but to collect. However, I do not want this lad's visit to the capital to disappoint him. There will be no contribution from you this night. I shall not even relieve Mr. Preacher of the guineas he has in his shoes."

Mr. Holker shook visibly; the highwayman laughed. "Now drive on."

At this he turned and disappeared into a grove of trees nearby.

The driver whipped up his horses and drove off in terror leaving the three of us standing in the dust of the roadside. In spite of shouted threats and entreaties from us, he would not stop. Thus we had, perforce, to walk into Kenilworth to the Dog and Gridiron Inn. Here the landlord made us more welcome, and Mr. Johnson delivered the cowardly driver such a blow to his buttocks with his cudgel that the fellow had to eat his dinner standing up.

CHAPTER · 1 4

London

Mr. Septimus Holker did not board the London coach the following morning. He refused to travel with such heathen companions as Mr. Johnson and Mr. Gilbert.

The day passed without any undue excitement, for which we were all profoundly grateful. True, we lost a wheel near Adderbury and were halted twice by flocks of sheep, and once a fish wagon forced us into a ditch, but we were used to such things by now.

We spent the night at the Red Lion just beyond Kidlington. Mr. Johnson declared that there was nothing yet contrived by man by which so much happiness is produced as a good tavern or inn. The meal also pleased him. "In point of diet, George," he said, "we English live upon butcher's meat. In Scotland they eat oats as horses do here. In France fancy soups, fish, and fowl are fashionable, but they know nothing of such delights as pies, pastries, plum-porridge, or brawn. I thank God everyday I am an Englishman."

We left the inn at six the next morning. It was a cold day, and we hurried aboard the coach. Fresh straw was added to keep our feet warm.

As we approached London, the number of coaches increased. Droves of animals now followed us along the road. "These geese seem to have something on their feet," I said, leaning from my window.

Mr. Johnson moved his bulky frame beside me. " 'Tis tar, George, to preserve them from the stones on the road. Many flocks of geese and turkeys are driven a hundred miles to be slaughtered at Smithfield Market."

Finally we were traveling along Oxford Street. Houses were built far enough apart to permit coaches to pass along the streets, but above us they jutted out, in some places almost blocking out the sky. As for the people, it was as if an ant heap had been kicked over.

The pavement consisted of round stones and the coach rattled whenever the driver had an opportunity to whip up the horses. Most of the time, however, we moved at a snail's pace. The cobblestones of the pavement were often broken up leaving small puddles of mud. Each time a wheel fell into one, the coach was jolted.

Large signs creaked above shop doors. One of them was a large grinning cat. Mr. Gilbert saw my astonishment.

"No, George, it isn't a cat shop. 'Tis a cheese merchant's. That is a Cheshire cat, and Cheshire, as you know, is a fine county for cheese. Don't be surprised to find shops whose signs bear no relation to their owner's trade.

When shops are sold, as likely as not, the signs are left. You see that one over there with *Tempus Fugit* on it?"

"Aye, sir."

"That means "Time Flies," but the owner does not sell clocks and watches anymore. If you look in the bow windows you will see that he sells perukes."

And sure enough, as we passed I saw dozens of wigs gazing back at me from their wooden blocks.

"I like these old signs," said Mr. Johnson, his body twitching, "but many are old with rusty hinges, and there have been occasions when one or two fell near enough to me to give me pause. However, their main use is in directing people to a certain establishment in a street. All one needs to say is 'near the sign of the Cheshire Cat in such-and-such a street,' and anyone may find his way."

"Why not number the doors?" I asked.

"Number the doors!"

"Aye, sir. Then anyone could find out where someone lived."

"Why, he can do that now, lad," replied Mr. Johnson. "Number each door—ridiculous. No Englishman could tolerate the loss of liberty. You've a lot to learn about the stout heart of the Londoner."

He sat silent for some minutes, then he muttered to himself more than to us, "I hope the driver has the wits to avoid Covent Garden, 'tis the worst crowded place in town." Leaning out the window he shouted, "Take Drury Lane and watch the luggage." He pulled his head in.

"There are many rogues and thieves in this city, for all I told Mr. Septimus Holker. They will steal the luggage if it falls off. The bolder spirits have been known to 'touch the rattler' or 'fly the basket' by jumping onto a coach from behind and throwing the boxes down to confederates."

Mr. Gilbert lit his pipe; and for once I was grateful, for the smell of tobacco was an improvement on the street odors.

When the streets narrowed, there was a lining of timber up to the height of the wagon wheels. This protected the houses and wheels; but it left no space for those going on foot. Consequently, they were forced from the wall into the center, where the channel filled with stinking refuse held pride of place.

"There on your left is Russell Street and the front of Drury Lane Theatre," said Mr. Johnson. " 'Tis almost ten years to the day that my tragedy of *Irene* was played there. It did not please the multitude."

" 'Twas caviar to the general," I added.

"You have read Shakespeare's *Hamlet,* George?" He asked in surprise.

"Oh yes, sir. I was a traveling actor once."

"Indeed. Tu-tu-tu," he muttered, while thinking this over. "I had found it hard to think of you as a coal miner."

"I am accounts keeper to his grace. I don't win coal."

"And do you prefer to work with your brain?"

"Yes, sir, I do."

"So do I, George. There's nought wrong with manual labor, but I agree with you—'tis more interesting if the mind's engaged. Yet we must respect physical work. My father, God rest his soul, kept a bookstall. One day when he was ill, he asked me to go in his stead. I was too proud. Years later, as a penance, I stood in the rain on the very spot where his stall stood."

"I so long to know my father, Mr. Johnson, but we were parted long before I was old enough to have any memory of him."

Mr. Johnson looked out of the window and lightly tapped the side of the carriage with his stick. Mr. Gilbert sat lost in his own thoughts.

"Depend upon it, George, there is a reason behind your separation and a purpose. We must all humble ourselves before God's Will and avoid the great sin of pride."

"Do you think I am too proud, sir?"

"I do not, but bear in mind the temptation to scorn those unlike you."

"I know what you mean. I lodge with a lady and her daughter, Peg. She scorns book-learning and such."

"Does she now," he said, rearranging the cushions behind him. "And why is that, do you think?"

"She despises me, of course."

"Is she about your age, George?"

"As far as we can tell."

"Then be advised by me. She affects scorn because 'tis the only way she can appear thy equal. There is no way she can get an education like your own unless you help her. Many appear to scorn what they would most like to have."

I hadn't thought of that. I was thinking of what to

say when a strange sight caught my eye through the carriage window. Across the street, in the middle of London, was a miner, black from head to toe. "Look at that," I said, "a miner in the center of London."

Mr. Johnson looked at me in amazement. Then his jaw dropped. He began to shake as if in convulsions; his whole body quaked; he laughed until the tears ran down his face.

When he finally gained control over himself, he explained, between gasps, "That is not a miner. He is a Negro. His skin is naturally black."

"Black?" I said in surprise.

"Aye. There are whole countries of black men. Why, there are countries like the Americas where men are red, and some, 'tis said, where they are yellow."

Mr. Johnson had a strange sense of humor, but I was not at all taken in by his foolishness.

He and Mr. Gilbert were still chuckling to themselves when the coach finally pulled into the yard of the Golden Cross on the Strand. Mr. Johnson watched the luggage as it was unloaded and transferred to our rooms. The innkeeper, a merry fellow by the name of Bruster, urged us to step into the coffee room and take a glass of something.

I did not get to take a glass of anything. Mr. Gilbert ordered me a mug of chocolate. Mr. Johnson and he took wine and then decided to lunch together. I had never met anyone who could tell such a good story as our new friend.

We had to part at last. But the day ended on a strange note—a disturbing one. As the coach bearing Mr. Johnson left the inn yard, I felt someone was watching me. Turning quickly, I was just in time to see a narrow face pull back behind a coach. It was over in a trice; yet I was sure of one thing. In this vast city, there was one who did not wish me well.

CHAPTER · 15

A Castle in the Air

I slept fitfully, for London was noisy even at night. The watchman took a delight in standing under my window and shouting the hour. It was a relief to rise at seven and eat breakfast, which was served in a private room.

To my great joy, Mr. Brindley was present. He greeted me warmly and assured me that Sal was well. He darted a glance at Mr. Gilbert as he said this, but the duke's agent had problems of his own. A flying barber had been called, and he was busy with his soap and hot water upon the agent's face.

Mr. Brindley was eating nothing, and occasionally he winced as if in pain.

"What is it, sir?" I asked.

"'Tis nothing, George," he replied, "a little toothache."

"A little," said Mr. Gilbert, now released from the hot water and razor and directing me to the barber, "why man you've been in agony this last half an hour."

"Maybe so," replied the engineer, "but fear not, for if it spites me, why I'll spite it. Do y'see, I have this hot chocolate on my right and this cold water on my left. When the tooth starts paining me, I use one after the other."

He clapped his great hand on my shoulder. "But hurry lad, you and me must go before a parliamentary committee today."

Then he let out a groan and slapped his hand to his jaw.

" 'Tis at me again," he said, reaching for the chocolate with his right hand and the water with his left.

At that moment there was a knock at the door. Mr. Gilbert opened it.

"Wait, Brindley," he said. "Here is Mr. Robert Craft, a blacksmith. I took the liberty of sending for him when I heard of your suffering. He often draws teeth."

Mr. Craft was a huge man. He still wore his leather apron. Without saying a word, he reached into the bag he carried and drew out an instrument that looked like a fire tong.

Even Mr. Brindley paled at this. " 'Tis nothing really," he began, but Mr. Gilbert had already brought up a chair and was pressing him into it.

"Perhaps after the committee meets . . ."

Mr. Craft peered into the engineer's mouth. Then with the tong he tapped a tooth. There was a roar of anguish from his victim.

"Inflamed," grunted the blacksmith. "Open wide."

He motioned to Mr. Gilbert and me. "If you please."

Mr. Brindley, seeing there was naught for it but to suffer, grasped the arms of the chair as we held him at the shoulders.

The drawers were fastened around the raging tooth—this alone caused the engineer great suffering.

"Steady," said the tooth-drawer. "And one."

He pulled the drawers giving them a twist at the same time. There was a bellow of pain from Mr. Brindley, who rose from the chair even though we were both holding him down.

"And two," said Mr. Craft, pulling once more.

It took four pulls; I felt each one of them. But at last, the tooth was out. I returned to the barber's chair.

"An eyetooth, with but one fang," said the blacksmith, " 'twill be a while before the swelling passes, but the ache is gone for good."

" 'Tis better already," said Mr. Brindley, "for nothing is so bad as a raging tooth." And he presented the blacksmith with two shillings and a glass of chocolate.

After this, none of us had much appetite. We preferred to sip chocolate from the silver pot and try to forget the blacksmith's visit.

Soon after the duke himself entered. Gone were the old clothes he wore in Worsley. Aubrey, at last, had dressed his master like a peer of the realm. But there was none of the haughtiness of a Lord Strange about him. His grace joined in the hand-shaking and back-slapping as unaffectedly as ever. Briefly, I wondered if my own father had been a man of education and breeding or a common laborer. Did I feel a twinge of guilt in hoping for the former?

"A glass of chocolate, if you please, Icarus," said his grace. "And stop daydreaming. There's dirty work afoot this day."

I poured him a large, steaming glass of chocolate. He looked around. "Why this breakfast is scarcely touched. Brindley, I thought thy teeth would have demolished that venison pastry, or is thy waistcoat button at the danger mark?"

Mr. Brindley managed a weak smile. It was his custom to eat heartily. When his expanding stomach raised his third waistcoat button to a certain place opposite his jacket he refused to eat a morsel.

"But I discovered at my stepfather's that people of quality take little for breakfast nowadays," the duke continued, drawing a chair up to the table. "If Icarus will cleave me a slice of that haunch of beef beside him, I shall be his humble servant."

Since we all knew how he would grumble when he received the reckoning, we were anxious he should eat as much as possible. We waited upon him like servants.

"Tea is being served at breakfast in some households," he said between mouthfuls, "but I prefer ale like any good Christian. Imagine," he added, lifting a tankard to his lips, "drinking a concoction of dried leaves and boiling water after it has become cold. A man can scarce get his hand around those heathen porcelain cups. No, 'tis a dangerous habit. Lady Montagu assures me that the very chambermaids have lost their bloom by sipping tea. She has a scullery maid who swears 'twas tea got her with child."

No one said anything, which surprised him. He looked from one to another of us.

"Of course, I don't believe that," he added, "but this tea drinking is a fad. Mark my words, 'twill pass. The people of England will never take to tea as they do chocolate."

Mr. Brindley spoke. "With your permission, duke, I'll withdraw to prepare for the committee meeting."

"Aye, aye, Brindley, I want nothing to go wrong this day."

The engineer left, and the duke gave the breakfast undivided attention for fifteen minutes. He requested us to join him on several occasions, but somehow we had no stomach for the coddled plovers' eggs, fish, cold beef, white bread, and fruit.

At last he seemed satisfied, pushed back his plate, and signed to me to pour him another glass of ale.

"Thankee, Icarus. Now," he said turning to us, "let me tell you I've not been idle these last two days. 'Tis the very devil to make men see justice; it has cost me a king's ransom to ensure that the right will prevail. And still there's no guarantee of success unless Brindley can somehow explain to a committee of pig farmers and tradesmen how to build a canal.

"And," he confided, leaning closer to us as if he

feared eavesdroppers, "I find Lord Strange and the Old Navigators have made much headway with the committee and some of the lords have wavered. In the House of Commons, I have fewer friends and even less influence. Should Brindley fail, all is lost, but don't tell him that. I want him to be himself. 'Tis true I have in my employ Gilbert's brother-in-law, Mr. Bill, but I have only so much cash—far less after I pay for this breakfast I'll warrant—to spend on educating members of Parliament that—" He broke off in amazement as the door opened.

There stood Mr. Brindley, the duke's consulting engineer. We all rose to our feet. "My God, Brindley," said his grace, "you look like an exquisite."

The bulky engineer grinned foolishly. He had abandoned his dull brown suit, waistcoat, and worn-out shoes and stood before us in new breeches of deep green, a fine embroidered broadcloth waistcoat, and coat with silver buttons. He had new shoes with matching silver buckles and a brand new black tricorne hat with gold edging and an ostrich feather.

"You said I was to dress well, duke."

"Indeed I did, Brindley, but I . . ."

"The breeches cost a guinea, the coat and weskit two, the shoes six shillings," said the engineer proudly. "I put them on your grace's account."

The duke took it well. "We must spend brass to make brass," he agreed faintly.

Mr. Brindley fished in his pocket and drew out a hundred pound note. "This is from your tailor, duke, to help on the canal, and this"—he drew out another—"is from a gentleman I met near Derby. He is in the pottery business. I showed him a way to burn flintstones to a fine white powder while I was there. I learned it of an ostler who poulticed Sal's eyes with it. He seemed to think it was valuable. The hundred pound was for me, but I might as well loan it to you now, since no doubt 'twill be yours sooner or later."

The duke carefully folded the notes in his pocket book. "Thankee, Brindley, you know how much I can use them."

A few minutes later the landlord informed us that a coach was waiting, and we were soon passing along the Strand to Westminister.

"The committee meets in St. Stephen's Chapel," said the duke. "Since this is a Commons committee, Strange and I won't be admitted. The chairman, Alderman Dickerson, is a fair man, but the Old Navigators will be represented by a very clever, shifty fellow by the name of McGinnon. He is a Scots lawyer of the worst type. His manner is to set all alaughing and reduce the argument to jest. But for all that, this is serious business."

When Mr. Gilbert and I entered the committee room it was already packed. There were hisses and jeers as we entered. A large, fat man in a lawyer's gown pointed to Mr. Brindley, slapped his knee and roared with laughter.

Most of the committee members had dress coats and wore their hair in bags; those that did not wore cloth coats trimmed with narrow gold lace, white waistcoats,

and had short, thick queues with curls on each side of
their heads. They didn't look like men who would be familiar with making canals and winning coal.

"All rise!" cried an usher as the chairman, Alderman
Dickerson, entered and took his seat at the head of the
long table.

"Is Mr. James Brindley present?"

Mr. Brindley stepped up to the end of the table.

"You are James Brindley, consulting engineer to His
Grace, Francis, Third Duke of Bridgewater?"

"I am."

The chairman looked closely at Mr. Brindley. "Those
are not the clothes you wear while consulting, are they?"

"Nay, sir, they are not, but in this company—"

"Thank you, Mr. Brindley, we are honored." There
was laughter at this, but it seemed in our favor. "Please
tell us what his grace plans to do."

"Aye. To build a navigable canal from Worsley to
Manchester, carrying it over the River Irwell at a place
called Barton."

There were hoots of laughter from Lord Strange's
supporters. The Alderman banged his gavel to silence
them.

"And how will you cross the Irwell?" the chairman
asked.

"By an aqueduct two hundred yards in length, twelve
wide, the center part being suspended by a bridge of three
semicircular arches, the middle one of sixty-three feet
span."

By now most of the committee members were smiling in disbelief. Mr. Brindley continued, "The canal to be thirty-nine feet above the Irwell. Even the tallest sailing ships will be able to pass under without lowering their masts—summat they cannot do at London Bridge."

There was open laughter now; some of it came from committee members.

"Thank you, Mr. Brindley, you may sit. There will be questions later."

Mr. McGinnon, the man in the lawyer's gown who had been so amused at Mr. Brindley's appearance, rose. He was a convincing speaker. Many members were soon nodding in agreement as he listed the main objections. He produced maps, handed out charts, and discussed lists of figures. He painted a picture of the duke as a madman determined to drag everyone and everything into his mad canal scheme.

When he sat down, I could tell he had done much harm to our case. Mr. Gilbert looked grim.

It was a somber group of us that sat in the Ship Tavern. Mr. Brindley hardly touched his pork pie.

" 'Tis not going well," he admitted, "I sent to the duke to tell him so, and he is meeting all the members of Parliament he can. But if the vote goes against us here, 'tis all lost. The duke will be ruined. He didn't tell me that, but I know."

He stared gloomily at his plate. "That McGinnon is a slippery fellow. He has a way with words. I feel things in my brain and know 'em to be right, but I can't speak 'em."

Things got worse that afternoon. Mr. McGinnon tried to make everything Mr. Brindley said sound like the ravings of a madman.

"What is the purpose of a river?" asked he.

Mr. Brindley replied without hesitation, "To feed navigable canals."

"And did God intend it so?"

"It seems likely."

There was more loud laughter at this, and Mr. Brindley looked puzzled. Alderman Dickerson was smiling too.

On another occasion the engineer stated firmly that "water, like a giant, was only safe when laid on its back."

When it got to facts, however, the engineer was well-prepared. Mr. McGinnon said many farms would be ruined or covered with water, but the engineer replied that a mile of canal took only an acre and a half of land. When the lawyer argued that mill owners would lose water, Mr. Brindley pointed out that this was impossible as all mills were below the eighty-two foot contour. Even Mr. McGinnon, he argued, would agree that water could not flow uphill.

Now there was laughter for our side. Very slowly, the balance was tilting in our favor. I began to feel better. Mr. Brindley was sweating and his wig was tilted over his left ear, but he was winning friends for the duke.

Then we received a nasty surprise. Mr. McGinnon asked leave to introduce a new witness.

"And who might it be?" asked the chairman.

"John Smeaton, the engineer, Mr. Chairman, Fellow of the Royal Society."

There was an excited buzz of conversation. Mr. Gilbert looked worried.

"James," he whispered, "why would they call Smeaton unless he were against us?"

"Fear not," replied the engineer confidently, "Smeaton will see the sense of what we propose."

"Mr. Smeaton," said Alderman Dickerson when he had sworn him in, "as England's foremost engineer, what do you think of his grace's plan to build a canal over the Irwell?"

In the whole room there was not a sound. Everyone waited to hear Mr. Smeaton's response. Committee members leaned toward him; I was sure my heartbeat could be heard across the room. Mr. Gilbert clenched his fists; his knuckles were white.

Mr. Smeaton turned to face Mr. Brindley and replied contemptuously, "I have often heard of castles in the air, but never saw where any of them could be erected."

There was pandemonium. The Old Navigators and their Tory friends leapt to their feet and applauded. Mr. Smeaton was slapped on the back and carried from the room on the shoulders of two brawny laborers. Mr. Gilbert's face was ashen.

"It's all over, James," said the agent. "The duke's finished. We have lost everything."

"Have we, by God?" said the engineer, lumbering to his feet and taking a half-guinea from his pocket. "We'll see about that. George, fetch me a cheese!"

CHAPTER · 16

Stop Thief!

On another day in London, there would have been cheese for sale in every other shop, but I went almost two miles until I found a cheese merchant in Greycoat Place. I gave him Mr. Brindley's coin, and he gave me a round Stilton cheese as big as a cart wheel.

"This thing weighs more than a basket of coal." I grunted as the merchant heaved it on my back.

It was over half an hour before I found my way back into the committee room. A semblance of order had been restored; all the parties were present except Mr. Gilbert.

Many curious stares greeted me as I handed my burden over to the engineer. He used his penknife to split the giant cheese into two half moons.

"Where's Mr. Gilbert?" I asked.

"Gone for puddle, George."

"Puddle?"

"Aye, we're going to need it. He sent to the river for clay and has two lads fetching sand and water. Ah, here they come now."

Mr. Gilbert and two lads came in carrying several pails between them. The agent joined us at the far end of the table. Mr Brindley cleared a space and then spoke.

"If you please, chairman, I have prepared an ocular demonstration."

"Indeed," said Alderman Dickerson.

"Aye. Ye'll see this cheese that I've cut in half. It represents the aqueduct supports." He placed them end to end with the round sides down.

He took one of the pails. "Here I have sand and clay." He tipped a little on the table. "If I pour water over it, 'twill flow away." He took a jug of water from the table, poured it on the mix, and it went everywhere. One member had to scramble to avoid a dousing.

"But if I puddle it," he added, kneading the sand and clay thoroughly, " 'twill hold water."

He formed a trough sealed at each end and carefully poured water in it from one of the pails. "Now behold," he said with the air of a professional magician.

Every eye was now on the trough of water. Not a drop leaked out. "Thus it is with canals." He lifted the trough carefully. It sagged a little in the middle, but it held. "And this is how I carry water over rivers." So saying, he laid the trough on top of the two halves of cheese.

There was a long silence, then a gale of applause. After that demonstration the committee would have given him anything he asked. They pressed forward to look at the model and to shake the engineer's hand. Alderman Dickerson took a vote, and with only one dissenting voice, the committee agreed to recommend granting the Duke of Bridgewater an act of Parliament to build his aqueduct at Barton.

I suddenly felt very hungry. I had had no breakfast and no midday meal, so while the two men lectured and drew diagrams in chalk on the floor, I nibbled away at Mr. Brindley's "castle in the air."

Soon the Duke of Bridgewater became the talk of London. Everyone wished to meet him; many invested money, and it was several days before the excitement died down and he could join us for breakfast at the Golden Cross. While drinking a glass of chocolate he was leafing through the *Daily Courant*. "I see that Mr. Garrick is to play Richard this very night," he said. "I am resolved to take you all, including Brindley, if his native sensibilities will not be overwhelmed by a visit to a public playhouse."

"Well, duke," replied the engineer, "I've never been to a play, but I doubt 'twill please me."

"Come now, Brindley," said the duke laying down the paper, "where's your spirit of adventure? Is this the reaction of a man who will build castles in the air? A man who ruined a fine oak table with cheese and puddle?"

"Well, duke," said the engineer, his great face covered with a sheepish grin, "if thou wilt have it so."

"Capital," roared the duke with pleasure, throwing down the paper, "we'll send a footman to secure places."

At five o'clock we left in the duke's stepfather's coach. His grace was already inside. At long last I was permitted to wear my ostrich feather, but when I took it from the trunk, I discovered it had broken in two.

We made a fine group of beaux. Mr. Brindley was better dressed than the duke himself in his fine new coat, breeches, and matching waistcoat. He carried a large notebook in which to record his thoughts, for although he spelled like no one else, he was a methodical man.

As the coach threaded its way through late afternoon crowds, the duke said, "We shall be going through some of London's worst streets. And there is a new fashionable vice of the young men."

"Which is, your grace?" asked Mr. Gilbert.

"Going 'on the radan,' as it is called," the duke replied. "Formerly the young bucks contented themselves with unscrewing door knockers and carrying them off. Now they seek watchmen and steal their staffs and lanterns."

"They ought to be whipped," growled Mr. Brindley, "we'd never permit such behavior in the Peaks."

As we turned north off the Strand into Brydges Street, the coach slowed to a walking pace. There were people everywhere. Many carried baskets of bread, fruit, or vegetables. Some hawked ballads or sold newspapers. Every fifty feet or so there were dingy, narrow alleys or courts leading to darkened shops. Creaking dangerously above people's heads were the familiar signs.

"A plague on all these crowds," said the duke. "If old Drury weren't so near Covent Garden we could get there in half the time."

There was a sudden jolt and those of us with our backs to the horses were thrown into the laps of those opposite.

"What now?" shouted the duke, helping me back to my seat.

"Thief taken, your grace," replied the coachman. "Ran right under the horses."

We all got down. A youth of my age, blood pouring down his face, was being led away by a burly fellow.

"Mr. John Fielding, the Bow Street Magistrate, will give him short shrift," said a gentleman standing by me.

"What has he done?" I asked.

"Done? Why, lad, you're new to the town, I see. He probably did nothing at all, but the fellow who has nabbed him is a professional thief-taker. 'Tis his word against the lad's. If he can pay a fine, the taker gets part. If he can't, and it's sure he can't, off he goes to Newgate Gaol or some pesthole like the Americas."

"But surely, not if he is innocent?"

"No man is innocent unless he can prove it. Never forget that, lad." He tipped his hat to me and disappeared into the throng.

We climbed back into the coach and a few minutes later descended in front of the passageway leading to the entrance of Drury Lane Theatre.

"Remember now," said the duke, "no hats to be worn in the boxes."

We entered the theater past an armed guard, to be greeted by Mr. Garrick's brother, George, who bowed low before the duke and said, somewhat grandly, "A signal honor for this house, your grace. Mr. Garrick wished me to inform you that he is most sensible of the honor your grace bestows upon him."

"Thank Mr. Garrick from me," replied his grace. "And further inform him that we have already heard that his performance in Richard has never been equalled on stage."

This was most unlike the rough and ready duke we knew in Worsley. To the left and right, people acknowledged his grace. Gentlemen bowed, ladies curtsied low. I was uncomfortable, and Mr. Brindley looked positively embarrassed.

The theater was much smaller than I had expected, and the continual noise was almost deafening. Our box lay to the left of the stage. Once the curtain rose, we would have an excellent view. Behind us were two galleries, each supported by six slender pillars. The upper gallery was almost as high as the ceiling itself.

We took our seats and the duke dismissed the footman. From the upper gallery, there was a constant uproar. One raucous booby was leaning over the rails and banging the gilt ornamentation below with a great stick.

From other parts of the galleries came loud blasts from a whistle that the duke called a catcall. Showers of orange peel and occasionally an orange itself fell on those below.

The orchestra began to play. The noise increased. The duke looked at his watch. "Third music," he said. "The play will commence soon. But look down there." I followed his gaze. There was a group of at least twenty young men wearing long flowing wigs of tightly bound curls. Their coats were festooned with ribbon loops, bows, and clusters. On their heads were tricorne hats with long ostrich plumes.

"Fops," said the duke. "Most come here to be seen, not to see. Some of them affect shoes with heels of two or three inches. 'Tis said many carry two watches in those elegantly embroidered pockets—one for telling what time 'tis and another for telling what time it isn't."

Several fops were staring at us through instruments held up to their eyes.

"Quizzing glasses," said the duke, who had also seen them. "The fops are great admirers of beauty, but a duke is higher in their estimation than any female."

The noise from the gallery had diminished slightly. Throughout the house, there was an air of expectancy; all eyes now turned to the stage.

Two servants in theater livery stepped onto the forestage with long candle lighters in their hands. From some of the fops came cries of "Snuffers! snuffers!" followed by loud laughter from their friends and hisses from the gallery.

Meanwhile six heavy iron rings, each holding a dozen long candles, had been lowered from above. The lighters swiftly lit the wicks. The chandeliers were hoisted up above the stage, and the audience stifled its chatter and clamor and became attentive.

One of the stage doors opposite us opened, and in strode an actress who took the center of the forestage and bowed low.

There was a thunderous applause. She spoke a prologue that flattered the audience while aiming a few lines at the fops. Then she was gone through the door to our right.

The great green curtain rose, and the play began. It was like magic. The theater seemed to vanish, and before us lay a huge stone room of an ancient castle. Torches in sconces on the wall burned brightly as the hunchbacked Richard, Duke of Gloucester, entered.

There was a thunder of applause. Mr. Garrick swept off his hat, bowed very low, and with the footlights flickering across his face spoke the venomous words of the evil duke.

I was swept up in it, and it was some time before I realized that my lips were forming the words even as Mr. Garrick spoke them. When Richard proposed to Lady Anne by the coffin of King Henry, I felt every word and gesture. This had been Mr. Winstone's favorite scene, and I fancied the famous Mr. Garrick had little to teach him.

So engrossed was I in the play that I blocked out all else until the first interval.

"Brindley, are you well?" the duke was asking. I turned quickly. The engineer's eyes were almost starting from his head; his face was positively green.

"Loosen his collar," ordered the duke, and I hastened to do so. Mr. Brindley drew in great gasps of air.

"Thank'ee, George," he gasped. "Duke, this play's too much for me. I never saw the like in my life. 'Tis too much. Should never be permitted. I'll never step into a playhouse again as long as I live." He rose unsteadily to his feet.

The duke was very concerned. "Brindley, we must leave. I'll get a surgeon."

"Nay, nay, duke," he replied. "'Tis the excitement of it all. If George will help me to a carriage, I'll return to our lodgings—no need for the rest of ye to be disturbed."

And so, with Brindley leaning on me, and accompanied by many expressions of good wishes, we made our way to the front of the theater.

A great crowd was milling about, and it was with some difficulty that I found a carriage. I was helping Mr. Brindley into it when someone bumped against me.

"Pardon, young sir," said a voice, but I was too busy to care.

Mr. Brindley settled into a corner seat. I began to climb in after him.

"Nay, George, thee enjoy the play, if ye can. Just tell the driver to take me to St. Mary's Church."

I gave the order; the carriage moved away. As I turned to step up on the path, a voice shouted. "My snuffbox. Stop thief!"

I turned to look. Not twenty paces from me stood Lord Strange and a skulking fellow with a weasel face. He quickly darted back into the crowd, just as a giant of a man hurled himself on me and knocked me to the ground. Strong arms seized me, and pinioned my arms to my sides. The stale smell of tobacco and wine swept over me.

My captor shouted, "I 'ave 'im, sir. Not to worry. I'm Jonathan Clements, thief-taker by profession. I've got 'im safe, sir."

"Let me go," I shouted, more embarrassed by the gathering crowd than afraid. "I have no snuffbox. I am of the Duke of Bridgewater's party. If you will send for . . ."

"Gawd's truth, listen at 'im," said Clements, " 'ow he do go on." He turned to Lord Strange.

"What's the charge, sir?"

"Stealing a gold snuffbox. It has the Derby coat of arms engraved upon it."

"I have no snuffbox," I repeated, "and I am no thief."

"Then you won't mind me searching you, will yerse?" Clements was leering at me through a mouth of blackened teeth.

"Yes, I will," I retorted, "but if that gentleman over there will undertake the search, I have no objection."

A man in clerical garb stepped from the crowd and placed his hands in my pockets, and within a few seconds he drew out, to my utter astonishment, a gold snuffbox.

"Well, now," said Clements, "this young gent seems to have his own snuffy."

There was laughter at this and a few cries of "Gi' us a pinch, lad."

"And his own coat of arms," Clements continued.

There was more laughter, and the crowd began to disperse.

I was stunned by the rapid change of events. It was clear what had happened; the snuffbox had been slipped into my pocket as I helped Mr. Brindley into the cab. I had been very skillfully snared.

A piece of rope was knotted around my wrists. "Now, young sir," said Clements, "if yer'll oblige me by walking, we'll be at Judge Fielding's Bow Street Office afore yer can say 'Tyburn Tree.' "

A fat woman with a yoke around her shoulders overheard this and protested. " 'E's just a lad. Let him give the box back. No harm's done. 'E don't look like no thief ter me. Look at his clothes."

"She's right," agreed a man in a silversmith's apron. "He doesn't look like no thief."

" 'E stole these clothes, like as not," roared Clements, "and ain't no one going to rob me of this prize cargo." He knocked the woman's yoke, and packages of butter, cheese, and fruit spilled on to the street. I was immediately forgotten by the crowd in the frenzy to loot the unfortunate woman's goods.

Clements heaved me on his shoulder like a sack of potatoes. Before the crowd knew ought about it, I was on the way to Bow Street Police Office.

CHAPTER · 17

The Blind Man
at Last

Once clear of the crowd, Clements dumped me on the ground. "Up with yer," he snarled. "Ye'll walk the rest." So saying, he rammed me in the back with his fist and hastened me along the narrow ally.

"Bow Street," he said with a grunt as we turned into a wider street with cobble stones. "Now, where's that stinking rogue Egan?"

No sooner had he said this than a familiar figure detached itself from the dark wall. He wore a tattered coat and a wretchedly filthy bag wig.

"Take the straw out of your shoe buckles, Egan," growled my captor, "I've need of a strawman."

"Always at your service," he whispered, looking me up and down.

Clements ignored him and addressed his next remarks to me as he hustled me along.

"You're a smart young feller, I can tell that. Now

this rat from the slimiest cellar whose bin followin' yer all over Lunnon is what we call a strawman. He advertises by the straw in his shoe buckle. For a penny he'll swear to anything. For two he'd shop his mother—if he had one."

"Then the magistrate will never believe him," I replied, "if there be any justice in London."

They both sneered at this. "Aye, put thy faith in justice if yer feel any better for doing so. 'Ere we are."

We crossed the street to a tall, thin house whose front seemed to be composed entirely of large windows divided into small square leaded panes. A large, fat water pipe ran from the roof and disappeared into the area in front of the building. Above the door was the number 4.

Most of those having business at Bow Street comprised as unsavory a crew as I had ever seen. Clements barged his way through the evil-smelling crowd and hurried me through a set of double doors. Egan followed close behind.

Before us lay a large, dark room almost bare of furniture except for some low wooden benches and the judge's great oak table standing on a raised platform at the far side of the room. Behind the table, mounted on the wall, was a large coat of arms. All walls were painted a dull brown and were bare except for a single picture of Liberty holding the scales of justice in one hand and a sword in the other.

"Sit there," said Clements, pushing me onto a bench next to a stout man of middle height, very sallow complexion, dark eyes, and eyebrows. A white wig was held in place by a dirty hat flapped before. His black coat was more shreds and patches than original cloth. He grunted and moved over an inch or two.

"Friend of Mr. Clements, are yer?"

I started to answer, but he gave a short laugh. "Well, if it's your first offense, you'll probably only get life."

"What have you. . . ?"

"Done? I'll tell yer lad. I snatched a man's watch."

"I see."

"I don't think yer do, lad. If I'd merely tried to murder the owner, 'twould have been a misdemeanor. Now, snatching a man's watch . . ." He sighed and leaned back stretching his arms. "That's a hanging offense."

There was a sudden hush. Outside the room, we heard the cry, "Make way for Mr. John Fielding."

"Up," said Clements. "Treat the beak with respect. You'll be first."

Everyone was standing and looking in the direction of a small door by the side of the magistrate's bench.

"This beak's a hanging judge," whispered Egan. "He'll settle yer, and right quick."

"Shut up, Egan," snarled Clements.

The door swung open and Magistrate Fielding entered.

Nothing I had ever imagined could have prepared me for the shock. My hands clutched Clements' filthy coat. The room began to spin. The magistrate was dressed entirely in black velvet with a black hat over his white powdered wig. A large gold chain of office was hung from his neck. In his hands was a long thin switch that he waved in front of him.

But across his face, covering his sightless eyes, was a narrow black bandage. I had come face to face with the man of my nightmares—John Fielding, the most famous magistrate in London. It was he who had pursued me through so many sleepless nights.

" 'Ere what's up?" asked Clements, feeling me fall against him. The room tilted before me, righted itself, then went black.

When I recovered my wits, a crowd of people was staring down at me. A cup of brackish water was pressed to my lips.

"How is the prisoner now?" the magistrate asked.

" 'E's fine, sir," said Clements pulling me to my feet. "Swooned from guilt, 'e did."

"All right, all right. Well, put him up."

I was dragged before the bench facing the sightless judge. A wooden rail some four feet high gave me support.

"Now what's the charge?"

"Stealing a snuffbox, Mr. Fielding," said the clerk.

"Gold, silver, or pewter?"

"Gold. It is the property of Lord Strange of Derbyshire."

"Lies," I cried, rising to my feet with an effort. "I stole no—"

"Silence, sir," said the magistrate. "We'll hear from you when I give you leave to speak."

Clements told his story; the strawman, Egan, vouched for the truth of it.

"Well, lad, what have you to say to that?"

"It's all lies," I said, "not a word of it is truth. The snuffbox was hidden upon my person by agents of Lord Strange, who seeks revenge because I work for the duke—"

"Enough of this," ordered the magistrate, impatiently drumming with his fingers on the arm of his chair. "I will hear no more nonsense. I have taken it upon myself to clean out this city. The snuffbox was found on your person, there's no denying it."

He smoothed the bandage over his eyes. "This is a serious offense," he stated, "and it must be dealt with severely. There are too many in this town who feel they can steal their way through life."

Clements shuffled his feet and muttered, " 'Ere, 'ere."

The magistrate ignored him. "No, young man. I shall make an example of you. You shall go to Newgate."

There was a gasp around the courtroom.

"And since stealing a snuffbox is a hanging offense, I doubt not that a jury at the Old Bailey will deal very honestly with you."

He rose from the bench and, feeling his way with the switch, left the room by his private door.

"Well, now," said Clements, "that's a rum go and no mistake. 'E's in a rare mood today. Something has gingered him up. That's very hard cos I was gettin' ter like yer. Now I fear you'll leaving this vale of tears at Tyburn Tree."

That was probably the only time in his life Clements spoke the truth.

CHAPTER · 18

Fever

I was taken by carriage up Ludgate Hill to Newgate Gaol by two Bow Street men. Three other persons, a girl accused of failing to pay a penny toll, an old man who had killed his neighbor's hog, and a villainous fellow who kept his face covered with the flap of a black cloak, made up the party.

One of the Bow Street men, a Mr. Hill, spoke cheerfully to us. It was as if we were on a sightseeing tour of the city instead of being condemned to the foulest prison in England.

"The city had seven gates, my friends," he said, "the gatehouses at Ludgate and Newgate are prisons. If you weren't in this 'ere carriage you'd see a carving of a woman and a cat. Now that there lady is Liberty and the cat is Lord Mayor Dick Wittington's. He left money for rebuilding Newgate. Not this one, o'course, it's not quite a hundred years old. The fan on top is ter help yer breathe inside. The jailers don't like to pay the window tax."

"Shut your trap," said the man in black from beneath his cloak. Our guide looked put out.

"Just trying to pass the time pleasantly," he replied in a hurt tone, lapsing into silence.

Soon we passed under the gatehouse. From the window grills of the ground floors hung collecting boxes. As our coach rattled past, I heard the plaintive cries of "Help the poor debtor."

Hill began fumbling through his huge greatcoat pocket; finally he produced a small coin. "I like to help," he said, leaning through the window and neatly tossing it into a drinking cup held out on a long stick. "I don't have much, but there are always those with less." Again he dug into his pocket this time producing a small, tightly corked bottle. Taking the end of his scarf, he sprinkled the contents of the bottle liberally on it. A smell of vinegar filled the coach as he carefully recorked the bottle.

Meanwhile the coach had halted before a great oak door studded with huge iron nailheads.

"Out if you please," ordered the other Bow Street man, a Mr. Robbins, heaving his bulk out first.

As we stood beside the coach, I became aware of the smell of rotting food and wrinkled my nose. "What's that smell?" I asked.

Robbins gave a grim laugh. "Ye'll find that out soon enough, lad."

Mr. Hill was hammering on the door with his stick. The grill opened.

"Four from Bow Street, three men and a girl, Mr. Reddish."

The grill slammed shut, and soon the door swung open.

A great wave of foul-smelling air hit us. Mr. Hill held his scarf tightly to his nose. The other runner quickly placed a dirty rag to his face.

"Whew! A bit fine today, ain't it?" asked Hill. " 'Twould turn the stomach of a horse."

The turnkey, almost as large as Robbins, stepped out. He had an enormous bunch of keys hanging from a broad leather belt. He looked more like a pirate than a jailor. A wicked white scar slashed across his face; he wore his own hair, a loose white frilly shirt, and black and tan riding boots.

"Gettin' a little fancy, ain't we, Mr. Hill?" he said swaggering out to look us over. "But ye'd better not come any further, we'll have the jail fever afore long."

"Well, then, if you insist," replied Hill, climbing swiftly back into the carriage, "we'll take our leave."

The turnkey gave a grim laugh, spun on his heel, and ordered us through the doors. They slammed behind us. We climbed up a flight of worn stone steps until another oak door barred our way.

"Before we go through," the turnkey said, "I'm the head turnkey 'ere. Mr. Reddish to you. If yer needs anythin', I can git it, at a price. Any you got chummage?"

"Chummage?" the girl asked in a weak voice.

"Aye, chummage or garnish. You can git gin or

even fresh water 'ere if you got the money. If you ain't, well . . ."

He left it at that, and selected a key from those on his belt. "Once through this door you'll never get out unless we takes you to trial, hanging, or the burial ground."

We followed him through. The stench was now so bad that the urge to retch almost overcame me. "The girl in here," he said opening a door. "You lot follow me."

We climbed up more flights of steps. "In 'ere," he ordered, thrusting me into a cell and slamming the door.

I stood in a stone room scarce eight feet by six. The roof was vaulted and just an inch or so higher in the middle than I could reach with an outstretched arm. In the upper part of the wall was a window, double grated, that measured two feet by one at most. The wall was lined with planks, each studded with broad-headed nails.

Three prisoners were already crammed into the cell. One of them sat looking at the wall; another nodded to me but otherwise remained engrossed in his own thoughts. They were almost part of the gloom and shadow. A guttering lantern gave out a dull red glow and filled the cell with smoke. There was a window, but it was shuttered from the outside and offered no ventilation.

The third prisoner, wearing a beard and covered with a torn blanket, rose and shuffled over to me on a pair of wooden clogs. "Welcome, welcome, dear boy," he said, "to our little home from home. My name is Judah Leigh. Do you, purchance, have any small coins with which to ease our passage from this world to the next?"

"I have not," I replied.

"Nothing, eh?"

"Not a penny."

"Ah, well," he said, and retreated into a corner, drew up his legs before him, and sat whistling to himself.

I sat in a corner fighting the urge to vomit; the door opened again. A turnkey entered bearing a set of leg irons and a hammer.

"Over there," he said, motioning with the hammer.

As he fitted the iron around my right leg he said, "O' course you needn't suffer the irons. For sixpence yer can git easement."

"Easement?"

"Aye. Them what 'as money don't 'ave to wear these darbies and gits to sit in the court instead of in here."

I had no money, but we soon agreed that my jacket was worth a shilling. I received sixpence and slept that night without leg irons.

The next day I was permitted to visit the court, and a more dismal sight never met my eyes. The felons' yard contained over forty prisoners in a space that could not hold half the number with any comfort. Some prisoners simply paced along the walls in a ceaseless journey that had worn a narrow path in the stones of the yard next to the walls. Some had partners, talking loudly and even joking; others walked alone, their heads sunk on their chests, eyes fixed on the ground before them. They never looked up, for what would they see but the walls, those grim reminders of their fate? A few men sat over in one corner drinking gin from flagons by their sides and arguing drunkenly over a card game. Others, men and women, sat staring at the walls, comprehending nothing. Two men, on their knees, prayed continuously. The stench rolled over me in a revolting wave.

An old woman covered by a tattered black gown hobbled over to my side leaning heavily upon a gnarled ash stick.

"Well, young sir, welcome to Newgate. What crime did you commit, if I may be so bold?"

"I committed no crime," I replied stoutly, "I am falsely accused of stealing a gold snuffbox, but justice will prevail."

She looked closely into my face. One of her eyes was covered by a white film; her breath smelled of gin.

"And yer believe all will be well?"

"I do. I cannot believe that this is happening to me."

She nodded sadly. "All you rats is the same. Use yer head boy. Why all around yer are cases of justice miscarrying a hundred times worse than yers."

And still nodding, she walked slowly away, her stick rapping on the stone flags of the yard.

Though I didn't know it then, I was a typical new prisoner. Thinking only of the time when help would arrive and boring everyone with constant speculation, I sought out the older prisoners and badgered them with questions about escape and deliverance.

I determined not to remain in Newgate a second longer than was necessary. On the second day, I found a potboy who agreed to deliver a message for me.

Overjoyed, I gave him the address of the duke's step-father in Piccadilly. "Just say I am in Newgate," I told him, making him repeat the address and giving him the sixpence.

The boy hurried from the yard; he had taken my only money, but I was not concerned, for wouldn't the duke or his agents secure my release within the next few hours?

The first night meant little sleep for me. All around me were the snores of my fellow prisoners. At times one would let out a shout or a scream of terror. Those who were next to him would seize him roughly and shake him awake. Muttering he would lapse into uneasy rest or spend hours waiting for the dawn.

On my third day, I was suddenly consumed with rage. The piece of bread I had been given for the midday meal was more moldy than usual, and I flung it down and leaped from the bed, hammering on the door with my fists and demanding a new piece. All the anger and frus-tration that had built up over the last days went into the frantic beating of the oaken door. Mr. Leigh pulled me away.

"Steady lad. The last man that did that broke a bone in his hand. And no one paid a snippet of attention." He led me back to the bed and lit his pipe. "Used to be some-thing of a rebel miself until I learned the value of going along." He cleared his throat and spat on the floor. "You get a bit unstrung when yer realize that life's got no rea-son behind it." He spoke confidently, punctuating each word with a stab of his pipe stem. "You'll learn soon enough, lad." He gave a dry, humorless chuckle. "We're all pawns, lad, in the great chess game of life. When the commands come down, there's nothing to be done."

"I'll never give in," I said. "Never!"

A week passed on leaden feet and then another. Mr. Leigh was taken away, and a new prisoner took his place. He was a tall, raw-boned fellow who never said a word.

Time became an endless chain of monotonous days and nights. I kept count of them by scratching a mark on the wall above my bed.

I sent a second message and then a third. To gain money, I learned the arts of surviving in Newgate. Whenever a rat—a new prisoner—was committed, I was among the first to empty his pockets for the precious coins that promised freedom and gave me the right to draw near the smoky fire that burned at night in the felons' yard. A sixpence meant that for a week I could eat bread that was not moldy and drink water that was only slightly brackish. Two more letters were carried outside by the potboy.

I lay on my bed for hours on end reliving my short life over and over again. It did not amount to much—parents I had never known, the terrible time at St. Dunstan's, the happy years with Mr. Winstone and his Sons and Daughters of Thespis.

I had been lucky in my friends, Mr. Winstone, the Duke of Bridgewater, his agent, and his engineer. I thought too of the cottage on Mill Brow and of Mrs.

Pendleton and her daughter Peg. More and more my thoughts returned to Peg. I saw her again in memory, walking briskly down the hill to the duke's mine, her canvas belt and iron chain slung from her shoulder. I remembered too her early dislike of me, her criticism of the duke's plan to make me a thrutcher at the rate of half a man, and the quarrel over the use of the tin bath. But the memories soon became too painful.

Slowly I became accustomed to the cell. There were times when I paced like a caged animal, fighting hard to restrain myself from shouting and banging fruitlessly on the door. But there were also occasions when I lay on the floor daydreaming. Dreaming no longer of escape but hoping still that my friends would assist me. There were strange moments of exultation when the lack of decent food and the monotony made my mind play strange tricks, and I would walk up and down the felons' yard sharing the joy that hermits must feel in their self-imposed exiles. But such moments soon passed, and I was again cold and hungry, waiting to hear what my fate would be, powerless, as Mr. Leigh had said, to do anything about it.

There was no particular moment at which I finally accepted the fact that I was abandoned, but at last I knew that no one was coming to take me from the iron grasp of Newgate Gaol. My friends had forgotten me. There was to be no rescue. In my misery I cursed the duke and all those who had left me to die friendless and alone.

Despair and anger were followed by a feeling of utter

wretchedness. I abandoned hope, and after two months, was unrecognizable. With no money to waste on water, I became indistinguishable from the filthy creatures around me. It was my daily habit to sit in the felons' yard covered by a moth-eaten blanket for which I had paid a penny. I bought it from a Middlesex debtor who preferred the warmth to be found in a glass of gin.

None of us was permitted soap or water, and no bedding other than straw was provided; and this was full of ticks, making life so unbearable, that many prisoners preferred to sleep on the stone floors without any kind of covering.

The food supplied to ordinary prisoners consisted of a three-halfpenny loaf of moldy bread each day. In the morning every man had a pint of gruel, at night there was a slimy broth made of rice and oatmeal. Very occasionally we had thin parsnip soup.

One morning, as I lay dozing in the yard, a hand shook my shoulder roughly. "Come on," said an under turnkey, "it's time for yer trial." Put on these irons and quick about it."

He led, almost dragged, me along the covered passage by the Roman wall connecting the prison with the Sessions House.

A jury was already being seated when I was fastened by a chain to the oak post of the huge dock in the center of the Justice Hall. I watched the last of the jury being sworn in and kissing the great black leather-bound Bible chained to an oak piller of the jury box. I was all too aware of the impression I was making dressed in rags and covered by a blanket.

Standing by one of the doors was the burly figure of Clements wearing a powdered wig and new coat and breeches. Near him, as filthy as ever, was the weasel Egan.

The Justice Hall was square and well-lighted. Tall windows reached almost to the roof. Above the judge's bench hung a blindfolded figure of Justice bearing a drawn sword. The pit of the court was full of scurrying lawyers in full wigs and black gowns.

"All rise," came the command as the judges filed in and took their seats. I looked a poor figure standing alone in the dock before the judges who were all dressed in rich ermine robes and long powdered wigs.

The Clerk of Arraigns read the indictment against me, and then an Old Bailey attorney rose, bowed, and addressed the Recorder.

"May it please your lordship and gentlemen of the jury, I am counsel for the king against the prisoner at the bar."

The trial was over in less than half an hour. The judges asked if there were any witnesses to my character. When I tried to tell them I had not been permitted to communicate with anyone, I was told to hold my tongue, for prisoners had no right to speak on their own behalf.

The chief judge did give Clements and Egan an uncomfortable time, but as I could not speak in my defense and was not allowed to see the evidence, there was little doubt about the verdict.

The judge also complained bitterly about the crimes perpetrated by young felons and instructed the jury not to be lenient on account of my age.

The jury returned in less than five minutes with a verdict of "guilty" and a sentence of "death by hanging."

I gripped the iron railing in front of me, but the sentence was a deliverance from the foulness of Newgate, so I did not lose my composure—though I was glad of the rail's support.

The chief judge took a black square of cloth from the bailiff and placed it over the top of his wig and said solemnly, "The law is that thou shall return to the place from whence you came and be taken hence to a place of execution. There to be hanged by the neck till the body be dead! dead! dead! and the Lord have mercy on thy soul."

For a moment the terrible words of the sentence caused me to shake. The hangman came forward, pulled my hands from the rail, thrust them behind my back, and slipped a whipcord over my thumbs and tightened it, cutting deep into the flesh.

I was taken back to Newgate, but I did not return to my cell or the felons' yard. Instead I was taken through a door on the south side of Newgate Street. This led to a large apartment on the ground floor, which was called the "Lodge." This was the taproom of the prison. Across the room was the entrance to the Condemned Hold; it was a heavy door on top of which was an aperture, protected by spikes. A stout prisoner in freshly powdered full wig, dressed in silk coat and breeches with a waistcoat of green silk trimmed with gold lace, was conversing through the door. A long rusty chain snaked out behind him.

The Condemned Hold measured no more than twenty feet by fourteen. There was one small barred window looking out into the archway. The floor was of stone and running around it, some two feet from the ground, was a wide wooden shelf. This was the bed. Two prisoners lay on it, heavy chains fastened to their left ankles. One was dressed in a black gown, the other in nothing but rags. He had a hawklike face; dirty patches of skull showed between hanks of unwashed hair. Occasionally he would clear his throat with a sound like thunder.

A long chain was fixed to my leg iron and locked to a bolt by my space. There was no easement of irons here. I sat huddled against the wall hugging my knees, for it was cold in spite of the feeble fire that spluttered in the grate. The smell was overpowering; putrifying fumes filled the air like a poisonous fog. I knew now why so few lived long enough to be hanged.

I slumped on the wide bench just as the finely dressed prisoner turned from the partition. For a brief moment we gazed at each other as if afraid to believe our eyes.

"Mr. Winstone," I said faintly, "can it really be you?"

"In the flesh, dear boy," he said, embracing me and kissing me on both cheeks to the surprise of all the other prisoners. "But George, would I had met thee in better times than these. But wait—"

He moved back to the partition; words were exchanged, and he returned with a bowl of clear water and a cloth towel.

"By your leave, George?"

I nodded, and he began to remove the dirt and grime from my face. "You did not know me the last time we met," he said, squeezing the rag and wiping vigorously.

"The last time?" I thought carefully. "Of course! Of course—the highwayman. You had a scarf over your face; your voice was muffled. You robbed us on the London Road."

"Robbed you," he roared, "robbed you! How could I rob you?" He flung the bowl to the floor and seized me in his arms, kissing me on both cheeks. "How could I rob the most promising actor in England? For George, 'twas I, Alfred Lewis Winstone, taught the immortal words of William Shakespeare. 'S death! I taught you to read, write, and reckon the few pence that was our meager sustenance. Do ye not remember?"

"Indeed, I do, sir. Those were the happiest days of my life."

"Aye, George. And mine too if the truth were known. But come, sit by me and unfold thy tale."

We sat together on the bed. Mr. Winstone took a bag of lavender from his sleeve, breathed deeply on it, and passed it to me. "Ah, lad, what did you do to earn the supreme penalty?"

"I was accused of stealing a snuffbox, but I swear I am innocent."

"Ah. George. In my case I was accused of stealing three gold watches, a porcelain snuffbox, three golden guineas, and a necklace."

"And are you, too, innocent?"

"George, lad, do I look innocent? Does a man dress like this unless he steals? The truth of the matter is I was insulted to be accused of such a paltry theft. Now, in short, I must take my quietus."

He took the lavender bag from me and breathed deeply into it.

"And I too, sir," I said, "though I had thought my friends would rescue me."

"They left you here when 'twas in their power to en-franchise you?"

"Aye, sir. I sent several letters, but they would not come. 'Tis hard to understand, for they seemed genuinely fond of me."

He took another deep breath of lavender. " 'Tis strange, 'tis passing strange," he murmured. "How sent you these missives?"

"Missives?"

"Letters, lad, letters!"

"By a potboy, a son of one of the guards."

"Zounds!" he shouted, throwing the bag of lavender to the ground. "Not that cream-faced loon Martin Tims."

"I believe so, sir."

"Dear lad, that explains all. He is a wheyfaced rogue, easily seduced by corrupting gold. Doubtless he took your money and burned the letters. Your friends did not desert you. As sure as I stand here they never heard ought of you from Martin Tims."

"Can it be?" I asked, joy and fear both nearly overwhelming me. I felt giddy. "They have not then deserted me. Even now they are searching London, are they not?"

"No doubt of it. But say, lad, who are these loving friends of yours?"

"His Grace, the Duke of Bridgewater, for one."

"Ah yes. I recall you were attendant on some great lord when we met on the London Road."

"I was, sir. But what of Mrs. Winstone and Cecelia?"

"I packed them off to the Americas. Mayhap some rich planter will marry Cecilia and knock some sense into her." Again he returned to the partition. I saw coins passed through. He was back soon after with a bowl of soup and a hunk of brown bread.

"As long as the garnish holds those in the taproom will see to it that we want for nothing. Yonder sneaking fellow is a veritable Iachimo, but his base soul will serve."

And indeed it did. From that day on we had plain but well-cooked food and wool blankets. There was even water to wash in. This good fortune was shared as best it could be with our fellow sufferers.

The prisoner in the black gown, a man called Mullins, expressed his gratitude; the others did not. "I was a lawyer once, and many a time I visited this pest hole," he said, "but I little thought I should languish here myself."

"What are you charged with?" I asked.

"Killing a swan," he replied. "I thought it was a pheasant."

"It seems hard," I said sympathetically.

"Nay, George. 'Twas vanity. I never would wear spectacles, and now I am paying a heavy price. I did have the pleasure of being taken in charge by Mr. Welch, High Constable of Holburn. I was committed by Mr. Fielding. That fellow is after a knighthood, mark my word. Before a year or two is out it will be Sir John Fielding." He paused and then continued. "But I did not arrive at this unhappy state without astounding my brother lawyers with my legal expertise. There were pleas, replications, rejoinders, surrejoinders, rebutters, surrebutters. Whenever a judge looked in my direction I put in a demurrer. I made legal precedents at every turn. But, in the end . . ." He stopped and looked around ". . . the swan won."

The other two prisoners said little, though they shared our food. Posthumous Nelson sat all day long without speaking, but, every so often he would clear his throat with a deafening sound like thunder. The other, a tall thin fellow with a blank socket where his eye had been, paid us no mind, and we left him undisturbed.

During the next few days Mr. Winstone cared for me devotedly. My strength was recovering, despite the misery of our situation, when there was a fearful change in Newgate. Those who had been there longest passed the word to the others. News traveled swiftly through dungeons, cells, and courts of Newgate. "The fever is here, the distemper is loose."

Everyone sensed it. Visitors stopped coming to the taproom behind the partition; turnkeys ventured near prisoners only when absolutely necessary.

"'Tis a fine revenge," said Mr. Winstone one day as we sat on the bed sipping a bowl of warm vegetable soup. "An irony that the great bard of Avon would have relished. We shall not die unavenged, for many who helped sentence us will die of the plague."

I did not share his satisfaction. The fever crushed any hopes I might have had of getting word to the duke. No guard would venture into a cell while the distemper was at its height. As for conveying anything outside, this was forbidden under pain of instant dismissal and severe punishment. While my execution had been delayed, there was no longer any possible hope of rescue.

And so we waited. Stricken prisoners were left until they died—longer if a turnkey decided the plague miasma was still upon them. The burial party came once a day. Many held vinegar bottles to their noses to avoid breathing in the pestilence, others held a lump of camphor in their hands and kept smelling it, still others crushed sprigs of rue between their fingers. But it was all in vain. Death stalked the corridors and cells; the death carts left every morning. Each day the rooms and walls were washed down with vinegar. And in the yard of Christ Church, the lime pits quickly filled with the bodies of the dead.

"Poor devils," said Mr. Mullins one morning as we heard the carts begin their melancholy journey. "I would much rather make my peace with Mr. Turlis's gallows than die in this cell of the plague."

"I wholeheartedly agree, sir," Mr. Winstone said. "All must die and a gallows is a fine stage. What actor could wish for more? An audience of thousands—not a paying one, 'tis true, but still a fine house for my farewell performance."

He moved close to me and took both my hands in his. "But I grieve for you, George, too young, too full of life to go to it. And never a tear, never a show of fear. 'Tis not natural."

At that very moment, I felt the tears run hot down my cheeks. "I am afraid, sir, I am. I don't want to die."

He held my face against his breast for a long time, stroking the side of my face with his hand.

"Nay, fear not, George. You have all the strength you need, but God will not foresake you. As for me, I shall hang because, in short, I deserve to hang."

But he was wrong. That very night, Mr. Alfred Winstone caught the jail fever.

"That's the end of 'im," said an under turnkey, keeping his distance. "An' if you gets near 'im you'll be gone too."

CHAPTER · 19

Flying the Coop

It had come upon him in the night; there was no warning. One minute he lay sleeping, the next he was sweating profusely. Then came the vomiting.

The head turnkey, Mr. Reddish, was summoned. He would not enter the cell, but stood outside holding a perfumed handkerchief to his nose. "Nothing to be done," he said, "'tis the fever all right. Put a blanket over him. He'll be dead by morning. The rest of you stay away from him."

All night Mr. Winstone moaned in his delirium; he tossed and turned on the wooden shelf, the chain and his leg iron rattling as he did so.

I took off my shirt and began tearing it into wide strips. Then I took a guinea from Mr. Winstone's purse.

"Bit early for that, lad, ain't it?" said the one-eyed man from the far side of the cell. "Let him die first; he'll be gone soon enough."

I ignored him. Moving over to the partition, I

shouted for a potboy. When one finally came, I showed him the guinea. "Fetch clean cold water," I said, "and a panniken, and there will be a mate to this for you."

He snatched the coin as if afraid to touch me. Biting into it he pronounced it "rum cole."

"Do as I ask, then, if you want its twin."

The potboy said nothing, but soon he returned with two pails of water and a panniken. I filled the latter with clear water from one of the pails and let it run slowly into Mr. Winstone's throat. Much of it was spilled, but he seemed to gain some relief from the burning fever.

"My second guinea," growled the potboy.

"Aye, you shall have it." I replied, "But not yet. I may need more clean water, and I don't think you will enter this cell in pursuit of a mere guinea."

He made threatening noises and cursed himself for being a trusting fool, but I knew that he placed a greater price on his life than one gold coin.

Night became day. I refused all assistance from Mr. Mullins for fear he, too, should be stricken. The tempo of life changed but slightly. Almost no food was sent in to us, for once the fever struck, the turnkeys would not enter a cell. Occasionally one would approach the partition, but not even gold would induce him to stay above a few seconds.

The potboy was more greedy. He refilled the pails of water and brought a loaf of stale bread and a bowl of gruel to us. The second guinea changed hands.

Mr. Winstone was worse the second night, and by

the third, we despaired of him. Black boils covered his skin, and when they burst, black tears ran down his face. His eyes were so puffed up that he could not have opened them had he wished. The lips were parched and cracked, though I dropped water on them all the time. The tongue lay black within his mouth. His breath wheezed and labored as it fought a great battle deep in his chest.

The other prisoners, convinced the Angel of Death would soon carry us all off, sat on the shelf as far from Mr. Winstone as they could. Once Nelson roused himself to speak to me. "Save your strength, lad, for he's not long for this world."

But I would not deliver him up to death. More water was brought, and I gently bathed his face. A third guinea purchased chicken broth which I managed to dribble down his throat.

I had no energy left. Four days and five nights I labored. In all that time I slept only three or four hours. All I knew was to keep him as cool as possible and to try to force food and water into his body.

But on the sixth day, the fever broke! The boils began to heal. They would leave scars in their place as a constant reminder of this battle, but Mr. Alfred Winstone would live to tell of it.

The breathing, once jerky and shallow, became regular and rhythmic. The swelling around the eyes began to go down, and the red bloodshot eyes returned to normal.

"My God," said Mr. Mullins when he saw the change, "George, I believe he's through the worst of it. Mr. Winstone shall live to hang."

When the turnkey was summoned, he couldn't believe what he saw. "It's a miracle," he muttered. "A bloody miracle."

If he said anything else, I shall never know, for at that moment I fell into a swoon and collapsed on the floor.

A hand was shaking my shoulder. "George, are you awake, lad?" I heard a voice say from a great distance.

When I opened my eyes, there was Mr. Mullins staring down at me.

"Help me sit," I gasped.

He dragged me to a sitting position, and I sat with my back propped against the wall. Mr. Mullins handed me a panniken of water.

"How long have I . . . ?"

"Two days and a night, lad," said Mullins. "It was not the plague though. 'Twas exhaustion. But lad, what a time we had with you. You had a dream and no mistake. I reckon it's a dream that will come true sooner or later. We'll all be on a cart going to a hanging at Tyburn soon enough, I'll warrant. Now drink this. Nelson got it for you."

From the distance came the sound of a throat being cleared.

I drank long and deep. It was cold, clear water. Then suddenly a thought came to me. I looked around desperately. "But where is Mr. Winstone?"

"Gone George. Been gone these two days."

"You mean dead?" I whispered.

"Dead! Dead? Nay, lad, gone. Flown the coop. Escaped."

"Escaped?" I said, unable to believe his words. "But how?"

Mullins refilled the panniken with water from a stone jug and handed it to me. "Well, lad" he said, settling himself alongside me. "When you fainted, we none of us could wake you. Mr. Winstone soon became himself and said we should let you rest. So we did."

"And?"

"He is a man of infinite resources. We're all to get two guineas apiece for our help. You can trust a highwayman; they're honest gentlemen."

"What happened?"

"Well, he lay down on his bed and cut his wrists with the edge of this very panniken. The blood he sucked up and left about his mouth. Then we told the turnkeys he had suffered a relapse and had died. They wouldn't come in, of course; he knew that. In the morning, the burial men picked him up and flung him on the cart. That was the last we saw of Mr. Winstone."

I sipped some more cool water. "But didn't the burial party check the body?"

"They never do, lad. They are not surgeons. They're buriers. In any case, we had him nicely wrapped up in his blanket. They didn't spare him a look. There were a dozen bodies on the cart already, and when they finished they had twice ten. One would not be missed at Christ Church. Mr. Winstone rode in strange company, but when a man recovers from the plague, he never catches it again."

Outside we could just hear the sound of the bells of St. Sepulchre's.

"And so there was no hue and cry."

"Not a squeak. The turnkeys were sorry to lose the garnish, but they wouldn't touch the body. Not even to search it for gold. Wouldn't have mattered if they had." He took out three guineas from his pocket. "We got three apiece with two more to come if he gets clear."

I got to my feet and began stretching my arms and legs. My mind was full of confused thoughts. I did not believe Mr. Winstone would desert me, but was there anything he could do?

"His last words were," continued Mullins, "tell George that 'Never will I rise up from the ground, Till they have pardoned thee.' Then something about a 'winged Mercury.' Does it mean ought to you?"

"I am certain he plans to prove my innocence," I answered, fighting hard to keep hope from swelling in my breast.

"Then let us hope he does indeed fly like a winged Mercury," said the lawyer, "for now I sense the worst of the plague has passed, and now hangings will begin apace."

It was all too true. In less than three days, the fever vanished as suddenly as it had appeared, and on the next I was called over to the partition. The governor of the prison stood in the taproom. "Prisoner," he said solemnly. "You are hereby sentenced to be hanged by the neck at Tyburn on Monday next in the year of Our Lord 1760. And may God have mercy on your soul."

Then he turned on his heel, and flanked by two soldiers, he left me alone with my thoughts.

"Well," said Mullins, "your friends 'ave four days yet to do summat in. Though I confess I can't see what."

I couldn't either, and as the dread day approached, what little hope I nursed dwindled away.

On the Sunday before the day appointed for my execution, I was dozing fitfully, when I was startled by the sound of a bell clanging outside my cell.

" 'Tis the sexton of St. Sepulchre's," Mullins told me. "He comes to the condemned hold at midnight to urge repentance." He chuckled drily. "'Tis a little late for that, I'm thinking."

The great bell of St. Sepulchre's now tolled the hour of midnight, adding to the din. Through the partition I could hear the sexton's voice as he recited:

*"Watch all and pray; the hour is drawing near
That you before the Almighty must appear
Examine well yourselves; in time repent
That you may not to eternal flames be sent."*

As his mournful voice died away, all those of us condemned to die knew that our last day on earth had arrived.

CHAPTER · 20

Tyburn Gallows

There was no more hope for those of us condemned to die at Tyburn.

" 'Tis cold comfort," said Mr. Mullins as he bade me farewell, "but the hangman, Thomas Turlis, has a new gallows. There is a drop that may make a clean break. But, kick your shoes off nevertheless. A man must die bravely."

Even the morose Nelson, who had scarcely spoken to me, came over and shook my hand and then retreated to the partition clearing his throat as he did so. It struck me that I should hear that sound no more.

I joined those who, like me, had clung desperately to the hope that bribery, influence, or reprieve would save them. Now, as we filed into the condemned felons' pew at St. Sepulchre's, still in irons, each was alone with his thoughts. A fat man in powdered wig sat on one side of me, great tears rolling down his face. His whole body was regularly wracked with sobs. On my other hand was a girl no more than twelve years old. She stared defiantly ahead.

Mr. Work, the prison ordinary, went from one to another of us urging us to confess and repent, keeping up a constant stream of prayers as he did so.

"I only stole a glass of milk," the girl told him, "for my baby brother."

"It was a grievous sin, child," he answered, "but God is merciful if ye repent and admit the wrong."

"But he was dying," she whispered, "dying in me arms." I heard no more as she was led away.

Apart from the snivelling fat man, the prisoners behaved with dignity. Though all felt the fear of dying, all tried to compose themselves. One felon was dressed in bottle green breeches, matching topcoat, new leather knee boots, and spurs. A huge white cockade decorated his two-colored tricorne hat. Lace cuffs peeped from his sleeves, and he wore white gloves. Seeing me looking at him, he winked.

"Well, young un, so this is it, eh?" His voice had a peculiar rasping note to it.

"It seems so, sir," I answered.

"Well, I'll let you sit next to me in the first tumbrel. You'll not blubber like that grocer, I'll warrant."

As we walked across the hall to the gate he added, "A man should be launched in his best. These clothes cost me a pretty penny. I intend to be hanged in better regalia than Lord Ferrers who was turned off a month or so ago a' wearing his wedding clothes. Of course, he was a lord and entitled to a silken rope. Well, *'aut Caesar aut nullus'*—'either Caesar or a nobody,' that's my motto. For us commoners, a hemp rope is all we get. But I can dress as well as he. Keep it to yourself, but I sold my body to the surgeons to buy these clothes."

We were being conducted from the Press Yard through the Middle Ward and along the side passage into the lodge. Here a vast crowd of debtors bade us farewell. "And," he continued, shaking several outstretched hands, "by God, I'm resolved to die game."

The lodge gate creaked open on rusty hinges. For the first time, the public got a glimpse of us. A loud cheer went up as the City Marshall formed up the procession.

" 'Tis a holiday today," said my companion. "The Londoners have us to thank for a day's entertainment that cost them nought. I should know, for I have made the journey before."

"Before, sir?" I said in astonishment.

"Aye, lad, 'tis not for nought that I am known as Half-Strangled Birch."

There was a sudden surge in the crowd and several people made us offerings—white caps with black ribbons, prayer books, nosegays, and oranges. Mr. Birch took a nosegay, which he fastened to his splendid coat, and an orange. The young girl and the grocer both received prayer books. I took nothing.

The City Marshall climbed into his carriage, which was a signal for the condemned to take their seats in the tumbrels.

A soldier climbed up into our cart, several pieces of hempen rope in his hand.

"I'll answer for the lad," said Mr. Birch. "No need to tie him down. He'll not jump 'til Mr. Turlis tells him to."

The soldier looked at me, nodded, and moved to another prisoner whom he secured to the side of the cart with a rope.

" 'Tis to prevent them jumping over the side," Mr. Birch explained, "but I take it you'll not disgrace yourself or me. All that's left now is to jump bravely into the next world."

I nodded.

"What's yer name, lad?"

"George Found, sir."

"Ah. Workhouse or Foundling Home, I'll warrant."

"St. Dunstan's."

"I know the place. So you're without friends or family to hang on your legs."

I shuddered. "Yes, sir."

"Well, today, lad, I'll be your father. Lean on me. It makes a difference, having a friend at a time like this. But come, make yourself comfortable."

He seated himself with his back to the driver and stretched his legs. "I insisted that grocer should go in the second cart, and I'll not share a ride with those two fellows in shrouds either," he added pointing to them.

A short, very dark man with piercing eyes swung up next to the driver. There was a loud shout, "Turlis, Turlis."

"The hangman?" I asked, unable to stop the shiver that ran down my back.

"Aye. Thomas Turlis himself," he said grimly.

The great bell of St. Sepulchre's tolled above us. In the distance other church bells responded. The last of the prisoners were being helped into the second cart.

A few nosegays were thrown into our tumbrel, and my friend knelt awkwardly and picked one up and tossed it to a group of servant girls nearby. He laughed as they fought for it.

All the prisoners were seated, most staring silently in front of them. Our coffins were now loaded and stacked in the center of the cart. Mr. Birch moved his legs until his feet rested on one. He looked more like a wedding guest than a condemned man.

A contingent of peace officers trailing pikes led the way. There was a jolt as the driver flicked his reins, the horse moved slowly and our cart edged forward.

"Well," he continued, as if nothing had happened, "I hit upon the idea of swallowing a metal pipe so the rope would not strangle me. I hung there for an hour before my friends could cut me down. I survived, but I could not speak for full two years after. Now Mr. Turlis is experimenting with a gallows that has a drop. He hopes to break our necks. More merciful he says."

This thought caused him to lapse into silence, and I was grateful. I wanted no more details of Mr. Turlis's gallows.

Behind us was a troop of soldiers in red coats and tricornes.

" 'Tis a fine sight," said Mr. Birch, recovering rapidly

from his depression and looking around with evident satisfaction. "A fine sight. And, if I mistake not, the weather
will not fail us. It would be a great pity if the last hour of
life were spent in rain or drizzle."

The crowd had so increased that their noise was well-
nigh deafening. Every window on Snow Hill was jammed
with spectators, and the roofs were swarming with young
men and girls.

We moved below on the cobbled street parting a sea
of the scum and riffraff of London. Every few yards stood
the barrow stands of gin-sellers. Ballad-mongers were
bawling the latest songs.

"My goodnight has already sold out of the first
printing," said Mr. Birch in his raspy tones. "It may equal
that of Jonathan Wild, the greatest thief of all time and
the first to escape from Newgate, our *alma mater*. I have it
by heart.

> My name is Half-Hanged Birch
> And that I'll not deny
> I leave an agéd mother
> In sorrow now I die
>
> Oh little did she dream
> While in my youth and bloom
> That I'd be hanged on Tyburn Tree
> And meet an awful doom.

"There's lots more, but it has a certain pathetic tone,
don't you think, lad?"

"Very much so, sir."

"Yes, true, true. I fancy many a pretty lass's heart will break on hearing it. I was to be a schoolmaster," he told me, "but there is scarce a living to be made at it, so I took up the high toby. You meet a better class of person, too."

The carts ground slowly up Holborn Hill. We passed the Church of St. Andrew's where throngs of people stared straight down at us from the steep roof. A few hats fluttered down. Mr. Birch managed to catch one on his head, at which there was a great cheer. He bowed to those high above us, which brought on renewed applause.

" 'Tis always best to die well," he said, resuming his seat. "When you are to die, dignity is all that is left to a man. On my last journey I refused to board the cart until I received the preeminent seat. 'Tis always a highwayman's by right."

I shuddered.

"Aye, lad," he added more soberly. "Ye'll see sights this day before you're cast off. Women dressed in black who come to carry off unclaimed bodies to the dissecting rooms. Then there are the sick who'll want to touch your corpse. 'Tis said a withered arm can be made whole if it is placed on the neck of a fresh hanged man. But look."

I rose unsteadily in the swaying cart. All the land on the right of Oxford Road was open country.

"That's Hampstead Church, lad," said Mr. Birch, "last one we'll see on this earth."

All the condemned prisoners stood holding onto the sides of the carts or onto each other. In the distance, by the wall of a great park, I could see a huge wooden platform mounted on four great piles, some ten feet above the earth. Rising above the platform were two stout posts with a beam across them.

"There it is," said Mr. Birch, "Mr. Turlis's new gallows. When he pulls his lever a trap opens and you fall through. But there is still nought to stop someone running under the platform to hang on your legs."

To the west rose a great gallery of seats, each one filled with an eager spectator. Many of the long ladders that I had seen lamplighters use were crowded with people hoping for an unobstructed view. Any courage I had oozed from me at this fearful sight.

"Don't look too long, lad, 'twill cause doubts to rise. You must leave this world for the next proudly. Not like that grocer." He shook his head. "Even the girl holds up better than he."

I looked at her; how different she was from Peg as she sat quietly in the second cart, her coffin resting only a few inches from her knees. It was impossible to imagine Peg accepting her fate so calmly. Indeed, I was surprised at my own resignation. Perhaps when all hope is gone, the mind is at peace. What was to be gained by violent behavior now? Mr. Winstone had failed; there would be no reprieve. I must jump bravely as Mr. Birch suggested. All that was left to me was the right to die with dignity. Yet I would have given much to glimpse once more the duke and his two advisors and Peg and her mother, even the cold yellow water of the duke's canal.

The procession was near to the gallows now; the

peace officers had to use the shafts of their pikes to clear a path. The cart jolted, stopped, moved a few feet, then finally came to a halt in the shadow of the gallows.

The crowd in the seats now grew silent as we descended. Mr. Turlis had already climbed onto the platform. A great cheer went up. He waved a stubby pipe and scrambled up a short ladder to the crossbeam where he sat ready to secure our ropes.

"Look at the scum in the gallery," said Mr. Birch as he stepped down using the wheel as a stepping-stone. "Those young bucks will soon be paying the hangman sixpence an inch for my rope. The seats belong to the Mother Proctor. She's made a fortune at these turning-offs. I wish they'd collapse around their ears."

He stopped. Friends and relatives were now admitted to the carts to say their last farewells, while from the crowd came the sounds of psalms that, for a moment, drowned out the cries of food vendors and ballad-mongers.

In the distance, there was a commotion on the edge of the crowd as a rider tried to urge his horse through the mob to get a better view.

As we walked to the gallows, we were pressed from all sides. Some wanted to touch us. Mr. Birch very gallantly kissed several maids and bit into a cherry tart held by a woman selling black puddings, chestnuts, and the like.

There was a loud cheer from the crowd as a white pigeon rose in the air.

"The signal we have reached our destination," Mr. Birch explained as the soldiers formed a circle before the gallows to keep the crowd back.

The hangman's cart drew behind the gallows.

"I'll let you go first, lad, because I like you. By rights a gentleman of the road has precedence, but you may go first." He drew close to me so no one should overhear. "'Tis better so," he added. "Courage begins to fail once the turning-off starts."

Mr. Work stepped forward, took my arm, and together we climbed the steps. Coming to the end of his prayers, he uttered a final benediction. Mr. Turlis secured the end of my halter to the crossbar overhead, descended, and slipped the noose around my neck.

"When I pull the lever," he said in a low, whining voice, "the trap will open and down you go."

He placed a black cap over my head and face; I felt him adjust the rope around my neck.

"Do you forgive me?" asked the hangman.

"I do," I replied, "and may God have mercy upon our souls."

"Amen to that," he replied.

I should not live to see my sixteenth birthday. There was a slight tug on the rope to test it. The prison ordinary began chanting a psalm behind me.

"Ready?" asked the hangman.

"Aye." I said, kicking off my shoes.

From the crowd came a great roar of approval. Then silence. There was a violent crash, the trap dropped away beneath me, and I fell into the void.

CHAPTER · 2 1

A Debt Repaid

But I was not to die that day. As I plunged into the abyss below, my flight was halted as the hemp rope burned into my neck. Strong arms grasped me around the waist and held me in midair. I heard a loud cheer from the crowd, and the mask was pulled from my head. I was gazing into the sweating but delighted face of Mr. Brindley. Under us, and sweating even more than its rider, was a small black pony. They had ridden under the gallow's platform just as I fell from above.

"A reprieve, a reprieve," the engineer shouted, as he removed the rope from my neck. Dropping me some three feet to the ground, he drew a document from his pocket.

The High Sheriff snatched it from him, and Mr. Turlis, cheated of his first victim, descended to the ground and read it over his shoulder.

"Aye," said the Sheriff, " 'tis true—signed by His Gracious Majesty himself."

He turned to the delighted crowd raising his hands

202 / A HANGING AT TYBURN

for silence. "The boy is reprieved by order of . . ."

No more words were heard in the pandemonium that followed. The air was filled with hats, cockades, black puddings, and apples. The mob, once so anxious to see me hanged, now rejoiced at my unexpected salvation. The soldiers fired their muskets joining gleefully in the crowd's festive mood.

I was seized by several burly carters and hoisted on their shoulders. An impromptu procession with Mr. Brindley at its head, leading the weary pony, made its way to Oxford Road.

There, sitting impatiently in a carriage, were his grace and Peg. At the sight of me, she let out a great shriek and ran toward me, planting a kiss upon my lips. At this there was a thunderous cheer and she kissed me again.

"George, I feared we should not be in time," said the duke. "Poor Peg will never be the same again. Nor, I fear, will Mr. Turlis's gallows."

We turned to look. The joyful crowd was dismantling the gallows and carrying off the wood. "There'll be no hangings today," added his grace, "for every prisoner will find friends to help him to freedom."

It was several hours before the crowds dispersed enough for the coach to take us to the Golden Cross in the Strand. I was allowed a glass of warm punch while a hot bath was prepared. All listened while I told my story.

"Aye, we knew mischief was afoot," said Mr. Brindley, when I had done. "The duke had all of London searched, but not a trace did we find. Finally he left several fellows to search while we returned to Worsley.

"I feared the worst, George," admitted the duke, "but I wouldn't give up entirely."

"How did you find me?" I asked.

"We didn't," replied the duke; "some fellow, who gave his name as Mercury, rode up to the Hall. What he told me sent the three of us to London post haste. At great expense, I might add."

"Was he finely dressed and did he speak strangely?"

"He was and he did," replied the duke. "The fellow borrowed a hundred guineas of me. Asked me to send six to some unsavory fellows in Newgate. When I demanded some security, he gave your name and added, 'Press not a falling man too far,' or some such nonsense, clapped spurs to his sweating horse and galloped off in the direction of Liverpool by later accounts. Who was the fellow?"

"A friend, your grace, a good friend. I will repay the loan gladly."

"Well, all's one for that," muttered the duke to everyone's surprise. "John couldn't be spared, though he wanted to come. Peg wouldn't be left this time, and Brindley insisted, of course, on accompanying me, though he has no love of London. I am glad he did, for we could not get through the crowds in the carriage, and he borrowed a pony only just in time."

"Well, I didn't exactly borrow it," admitted the engineer, " 'took' might be a better way o' putting it."

The duke laughed and helped himself to a glass of punch. There was a knock at the door. "Ah, that will be my guest," said he. "Brindley, if you would be so kind."

The bulky engineer grunted, rose from his chair, and

opened the door. I heard him give a start of surprise. Then he announced, "Mr. John Fielding."

I rose to my feet. Before us, taking off a long black cloak, stood the blind Bow Street magistrate, his switch in hand. This was the first time I had seen him at close quarters. He was taller than Mr. Brindley by four or five inches, but thin, almost gaunt. The skin on his face was gray and like parchment. Below the dreadful black bandage, his cheeks were hollow, the lips thin and bloodless, but the most prominent feature of his face was his nose; it was long with splayed-out nostrils.

The magistrate's cloak was taken by Mr. Brindley; his waistcoat was plain and the buttons mere brass.

The voice had its familiar sharp edge when he spoke. "Your grace honors me with this invitation, but before I say ought else, I must take the hand of the young lad I so wronged."

He held out his hand. The duke nodded to me, and I took it reluctantly. The magistrate's grip was firm.

"I am a humbler man than when I last saw you, George. I'll admit that I was beginning to think of myself as invincible. When a man can recognize three thousand criminals by voice alone, he starts to think of himself as a god. Well, young man, you have taught me that might is not right and that justice must be tempered with mercy. I shall be a better justice in the future, and those brought to Bow Street shall have cause to thank you."

He sat in the rush bottom chair by the fire and was given a glass of punch.

"Of course, I still owe you an explanation. Perhaps if I had my sight, you would not nearly have graced Mr. Turlis's new gallows or assisted that damn croaking Birch to escape the noose a second time. For indeed, though you will bear a rope burn around your neck to remind you of our encounter, I am your friend not your enemy."

"Then why do I dream of you, and why do you seek me?" I asked, putting my glass down and sitting opposite him. "What have I done?"

The blind magistrate leaned forward in his chair.

"George, the imagination of a young child is a marvelously inventive thing," he replied. "I seek you at your father's request."

"My father," I demanded eagerly. "You know my father? Where is he? Who is he? Sir, I long to know."

"Patience, lad. My news is not all good. Your father is alive, though I am sorry to say your mother died many years ago."

I sat back in my chair and turned my face to the fire. "My mother dead?"

"Aye, George. These fifteen years since."

There was a deep silence in the room, then a piece of wood cracked on the fire, startling everyone. The duke cleared his throat, seemed about to speak, then changed his mind.

The knuckles of my hand were white as I gripped the arms of my chair. "And my father?" I asked, hesitatingly. "What of him?"

"Rest easy on that score, George," replied the magis-

trate. "He is Sir Robert Forster, the famous Bristol surgeon. When your mother married a poor doctor against
her parents' wishes, they disowned her. Your father went
to sea, was shipwrecked and believed lost; your mother
became destitute, but she would not apply for relief to her
parents, and so she made her way to London where soon
she was forced into a workhouse. Three months later she
died. You know the rest."

"But where do you come in?" asked the duke, refill-
ing Mr. Fielding's glass.

"Thank'ee, a very fine punch indeed, your grace.
Well, when George's father was rescued, he came home to
find wife and child vanished without trace. As his old
friend, and because I was familiar with police work, he
asked me to help. You may have seen me once or twice. A
blind man's bandage is a fearful thing to a young child.
And, I might add, to many a confirmed rogue."

"Where is my father now?"

Mr. Brindley took the magistrate's empty glass and
placed it on the table. Mr. Fielding continued. "The
events I speak of happened many years ago. Your father
finally accepted the fact that he would find no son alive;
he took ship to the West Indies or the Americas. He is a
surgeon. I have heard naught of him since and know not
where he might be."

The duke cleared his throat again, then began to fill
his pipe. Peg came and knelt beside my chair, slipping her
hand in mine. Tears were forming in the corner of her
eyes.

Everyone in the room knew that this was the bitterest disappointment of my life. To be so near to finding my father, to be in the presence of one who had known him and spoken of him. It seemed impossible that I should be defeated once again.

"Well," I said, trying to conceal my disappointment. "At least I can return to Worsley, where I have friends, a home, and a shilling a day."

But no one was cheered by this, and a large tear rolled slowly down Peg's cheek.

III

A Castle in the Air

CHAPTER · 22

Mr. Gilbert's Discovery

Five days later I stood again on Worsley Common. Remarkable changes had taken place in my absence. A warehouse was under construction; at the far end was a huge crane, which was already being used to lift goods from the bank of the canal into barges waiting below. The works yard was spreading rapidly across the Common, and there was a thick pall of smoke obscuring the top of the tall brick chimney of the smithy.

Leaving my horse tethered by the blacksmith's shop, I strolled to the east side of the common. A new row of cottages were being constructed. Masons, slaters, and carpenters worked frantically to finish one of the cottages. A woman and four children stood ready to enter as soon as the carpenters left. They would be sleeping in it before the tiles on the roof had settled.

Cuthbert Heaton, the duke's mole-catcher, saw me and strode over to shake my hand.

"So tha couldn't stay away," he said with a broad smile. "This's 'half-crown row,' tha knows."

"Half-crown row?"

"Aye, another of 'is grace's ideas. All those fined for being late or for what 'e calls 'dereliction of duty,' pays into a fund to help build them cottages."

"I suppose I'll have to collect those fines," I said. " 'Tis not a happy prospect."

"That's how come Peter Wearing got 'issel' thrown in t'basin. Why, George," he said, clapping a huge hand on my shoulder. "Tha could become a mole-catcher. It's pleasant out-of-doors work. Better than collecting fines. Important work too; moles do a lot of damage to canal banks, and 'is grace pays a penny a tail. And I gets ter keep the skins tha knows. I sells a few here, and some goes to Manchester and Liverpool. It's very useful for smoothing things. The skin lies smooth in either direction."

"How many moles do you catch in a day, Cuthbert?"

"Sometimes two dozen, some days more, others nowt. February's best o'course when plowing's done."

"Well, I'll think it over, Cuthbert, but as accounts keeper I am paid a regular salary, *if* there is any money, of course."

The mole catcher grinned, heaved a sack over his shoulder, and strode off whistling through his teeth.

I soon settled back into the rhythm of work. The duke wanted to start an action at law against Lord Strange.

"Damme, George," he said, "it was me he was after. But he knew he couldn't touch me, or Gilbert or Brindley, for that matter, so he conspired against you. Any decent Englishman would be thoroughly ashamed of himself for even thinking of such a scheme. Let me engage legal counsel."

But I refused. I wanted no more of Lord Strange. Besides, the way to defeat him was to complete the aqueduct, and that was proving no easy task. The land on each side of the Irwell was little more than a vast swamp. Cattle had strayed into it and been swallowed up whole. Yet slowly, as Mr. Brindley had predicted, it was drained and solidified with waste from the mine.

Once the engineer declared the land firm enough, digging commenced. The laborers were now called "navvies," a shortened form of the word "navigators." The duke was mightily put out at this and insisted that in his presence the word "canallers" should be used. No one paid the slightest attention.

"I tell thee, George," said Mr. Brindley one day as we watched the huge labor force toiling away. "When this is given over, men who know will praise these embankments through Barton Moss and Trafford Moss more than they will my castle in the air."

One of the secrets I quickly learned was that a wet embankment could be prevented from slipping by dusting powdered lime in layers over the wet earth. Unfortunately lime was very expensive, and the only nearby supply was Sutton Lime dug from a quarry at Astley. Our remaining supply came thirty miles from Buxton. As each load was delivered, the duke often supervised its unloading.

"It's going to break me, Icarus," he said groaning one day as I was casting up his accounts. "'Tis the last straw. I've faced a thousand problems and conquered, but lime is so costly and so necessary for joining bricks together that I can scarce bear to see it thrown onto the embankments."

He fussed in his waistcoat pocket for his snuffbox. I quickly made my excuses and left. As I hurried away, two loud thunderclaps rent the air.

The aqueduct fascinated me. Huge oak pilings were sunk into the bed of the River Irwell. The men worked inside a circular dam, using pumps to keep the water out. Those driving the piles struggled in mud up to their waists, hauling on great ropes that raised an iron weight above the piles. On a command, "Let fall!" they released the rope and the weight fell, driving the piling another few inches into the ground. This work was considered so demanding that I was ordered to allow two pints of ale per man per day. The sawyers, who had to cut and shape the piles, received half that.

The canal was almost to the River Irwell when a curious accident happened. I was sent by the duke with a message to Mr. Gilbert. Reaching the spot where he was supposed to be and not seeing him, I was foolish enough to set out in search for him. I had gone less than a hundred yards when my foot caught a tree root and tumbled me down an incline with much shouting on my part, though more in exasperation than fear. I ended up at the foot of a small hill amidst a shower of rocks and earth. Mr. Gilbert, who was nearby, heard the disturbance and hurried to my side.

"George, is all well?"

"My pride is hurt, but nothing else," I said, getting to my feet.

Mr. Gilbert was brushing me down when he suddenly let out a cry and went down on one knee to examine some of the rocks I had dislodged. Then he eagerly examined an outcrop.

"George," he said, turning to me. "Your fall has saved his grace twenty thousand pounds. This chalky substance all around us may well be the biggest deposit of lime in South Lancashire."

To say the duke was pleased is an understatement. He almost danced for joy when we told him. "Didn't I tell thee, Icarus, Gilbert is a man in a million."

To give him his due, the agent did attempt to correct him, but the duke wouldn't let him. "Nay, nay, John, credit where credit's due, say I."

That night there was a private celebration to which I was not invited. The next day I entered in the account book:

	£	s	d
Brindley (arrears in salary)	24	6	8
Gilbert (arrears in salary)	40	10	0
Wine (to celebrate Gilbert's discovery)	10	10	0

As if that weren't bad enough, Mrs. Perkins told me that the three men, while celebrating *Mr. Gilbert's* discovery, consumed some thirty-six Lancashire fat rascals.

" 'Twas a pity they didn't choke on them," I replied to her astonishment.

CHAPTER · 23

Disaster

Many people took advantage of the duke's preoccupation with his canal. I was with him one day walking down the towpath when a young lad accosted us.

"My dad say tha'll never have enough brass to finish this navigation," said the boy.

"Oh does he?" said the duke, reaching into the pocket of his brown suit. He took out a fourpenny piece and laid it in the lad's palm. "Well, you just show this to your father, and tell him that if he had as many fourpenny-pieces as the duke, there's no question he'd finish the work all right! And you tell him it's a canal, *canal,* boy, not a navigation."

The boy took the coin, bit into it, grinned, and ran off down the towpath.

At last the day dawned for which we had all striven so long and mightily. The surface canal had reached the Irwell! A crane, mounted on a large flat, could now be used to lower coal in stout wooden boxes from starva-

tioners to the duke's newly built river barges waiting
below on the River Irwell. But since his grace had to pay
the full toll to the Old Navigators, his coal was sold at a
loss.

The strain of the work took its toll. Fights broke out
among the men. Even the duke's right-hand men quar-
reled about the weighting of the arches of the aqueduct.
Mr. Brindley insisted on puddling the sides of the aqueduct more heavily than the arches.

"But James, there will be some eight hundred tons of
water in the trough. We must allow the arches to take all
the weight possible," protested Mr. Gilbert.

" 'Tis a matter of weight distribution," snapped Mr.
Brindley, who for days had done with only a few hours
sleep. He refused to discuss the matter further, and the
agent reluctantly let him have his way.

Layers of straw and puddle were carefully applied to
the stone walls of the aqueduct until they formed a clay
trough—a giant version of that which the engineer had
fashioned before the parliamentary committee not six
months before.

The aqueduct amazed all who came to see it. Three
arches rose almost forty feet above the river Irwell;
the center arch had a span of sixty-three feet. From end to
end the aqueduct measured two hundred yards, and it
was a dozen feet wide. The Barton Moss embankment
leading to it was half a mile long and seventeen feet
high.

"It is the greatest man-made curiosity in the world,"

one visitor said, watching a sailboat pass under the aqueduct.

"Aye," muttered Mr. Gilbert to me, "but it has not yet held a drop of water."

But surely, Mr. Gilbert," I said, "you do not think that . . ."

"I think what I think, George," he said abruptly, and walked away.

On the day that water was to be let in, everyone living in Worsley and for ten miles about journeyed to Barton.

Mr. Brindley was everywhere. There were great bags under his eyes, and I smelt liquor on his breath. The duke asked anxiously after his health, but the response was not encouraging. "The engineer would inform his grace on the subject of his health after the aqueduct had been filled."

Water was allowed in very slowly. Two sluices in the gate were raised a few inches at a time. Water foamed through the gap and entered the clay trough. All seemed well, and Mr. Brindley signaled to the men at the sluices to raise them to the limit.

All at once there was a loud cry of alarm from Mr. Gilbert and those standing by him. We all saw the reason. The weight of water was so great that the first arch had begun to buckle. The sluices were hurriedly dropped; the arch swayed back into position and held.

And never had I felt more anguish before or since for a man as I felt at that moment for James Brindley, the man who said water could be carried over a river. The man in whom the duke had placed his faith and his entire fortune. The engineer turned pale, began to shake, and then hurried away, thrusting himself through the crowd.

Below, on the banks of the Irwell, spectators scattered like chaff in the wind. Those of us on the far side were doused with water when more sluices were opened to let the water escape. Shouts, curses, and screams came from all around me. Parents searched frantically for children lost in the melée. Most spectators ran away from the aqueduct along the banks of the Irwell, but some tried to climb the embankment up to the canal. Many of these slipped in the thick brown mud. Peg was helping an old woman escape when she tripped and fell. Her bonnet flew off and was instantly trampled underfoot by a group of burly miners. When she stood up, her dress was mud from top to bottom.

It was well over an hour before the duke and Mr. Gilbert could restore order. There were anxious inquiries after Mr. Brindley, who had not been seen after the water was let in. We learned that the failure of the aqueduct had been too much for him. Excitement and nervous exhaustion had overwhelmed him, and he had sought his bed at Blaize Tavern. There he remained. He refused all visitors, even his grace, the Duke of Bridgewater.

CHAPTER · 24

Art Conquers Nature

The duke was the laughingstock of Lancashire. There were demands for instant repayment on some of the loans. Even those closely associated with the enterprise shook their heads and talked of "Duke's Folly," and Mr. Gilbert had to spend several days riding around the countryside to assure investors that their money was safe.

The duke put a brave face on it. In Brindley's absence, he took personal control of the work on the Trafford Moss embankment on the far side of the aqueduct, for he was determined to proceed as if nothing serious had occurred. He calmed many fears by announcing that none of the navvies would be turned off.

Mr. Gilbert took equally decisive action. Clay and straw were stripped from the aqueduct and construction of a huge new puddling pit begun. The great strips of clay were carefully mixed with water and pressed into fresh puddle. The weight was redistributed, and the weak arch was heavily weighted with clay while the sides of the trough were lightened.

"You see, George," he said to me as we watched the puddle being applied, "I always felt the weight should be on the arches. Eight hundred tons of water is a great load, and should it press too much on the sides, 'twould be like a great wind hitting the side of the aqueduct. That's what happened, and so the first arch began to buckle."

Those associated with the Irwell Navigation made no attempts to conceal their joy. Lord Strange himself, it was said, traveled down river to gaze at the suspect arch. His boatmen jeered as they passed under the center span and made a great show of protecting their heads from falling masonry.

Three weeks later the aqueduct was repuddled. Mr. Gilbert declared that the arches should be allowed several months to settle. Mr. Brindley still could not bear to look at "Duke's Folly" so he was charged by the duke to take control of the Trafford Moss embankment. His manner changed, however; he became morose and ill-tempered. When the men asked his advice, he told them to refer to "his grace's agent who is now in control of the canal." His spare time was spent in his room. When he came to work, all could smell the liquor on his breath. Indeed he twice lost his footing and fell into the canal. He was quick to take offense, complaining peevishly to the duke whenever Mr. Gilbert suggested a course of action contrary to his own. Once so popular with the men, he became a tyrant in their eyes.

One evening in the middle of September sometime

after the Harvest Supper, the Pendletons and I were sitting in front of the fireplace drinking chocolate and munching a fresh batch of fat rascals when there was a sound of a horse outside followed by a knock at the door. Opening it, I was surprised to see Mr. Gilbert.

"Good evening to you all," he said, entering and allowing Peg to take his hat and coat. He sat down before the fire and took a glass of chocolate.

"Thank you, ma'am," he said to Mrs. Pendleton, " 'tis a chilly night for September, is it not?"

He did not wait for an answer but continued. "I am come about Brindley. As you know he is not the man he once was. His confidence is gone, and I have a plan to help him regain it. But we must all swear to secrecy first, for should anything go wrong, 'twill do him more harm than good."

"What are we to do?" I asked.

"It's clear to me that Brindley weighted the arches wrong. Now the aqueduct has been repuddled, the weighting will help stabilize the arches. That bridge will last a hundred years. I'll stake my reputation on it, and indeed I have. But if Brindley were freed of anxiety of waiting until next spring to see if the aqueduct does hold—*if* he knew in advance all was well, think how 'twould cheer the man."

"Well I don't see what we can do," said Peg, looking up from the reeds she was plaiting into a mat, "we can't . . ."

Her voice trailed off. Mr. Gilbert had risen to his feet.

"Aye, we can," he said, "and this very night. You two will lift the sluices and let the water in. I shall watch the arch. If there is any sign of buckling we'll know the worst, but if it holds firm, as I am convinced it will, I shall have a quiet word with Brindley tonight at Blaize Tavern. Now are ye with me?"

We were. An hour later we stood by the gate at the edge of Barton aqueduct. The moon was full.

Mr. Gilbert scrambled down to the bank of the river some forty feet below us. When he waved his arm, we turned the handles that raised the sluice gates. Water escaped into the clay trough, bubbling and churning as it shot through the narrow gap at the bottom of the gates. Foaming, it raced across the dark clay lining of the aqueduct until stopped by the gate at the far end. Then it surged back over itself finally settling a foot deep throughout. After this there was little to show that water was still pouring in, but we could see the level slowly rising, and there was an occasional slap of water against clay to indicate that tons of water were settling on the arches of the aqueduct.

After thirty minutes, Mr. Gilbert climbed back to where we stood.

"There was not so much as a tremor," he said. "I did not see a drop of water fall from the stonework."

Then he walked along the towpath from one end of the aqueduct to the other, pausing occasionally to peer into the water.

"All is well," he said at length. "Now George, close

your sluice, and Peg, you open the other one. I want all traces of water gone before prying eyes appear."

We did as he instructed, then rejoined him. He took out his pipe and tobacco and filled the bowl, never for one second taking his eye off the falling water.

"We have seen something this night," he continued, puffing contentedly on his pipe, "that will change the future of all England. His grace, James Brindley, and we three have shown the nation that canals can be taken almost anywhere. Mark my words, you two, this is the most important event in the last hundred years. Art has conquered nature."

"It's cold," said Miss Margaret Pendleton, "I'd like some more chocolate!"

So much for glory.

CHAPTER · 25

A Stranger and His Horse

Mr. Gilbert went straight to Blaize Tavern to tell Mr. Brindley the news. I heard later that a great deal of rather expensive wine and two bottles of French brandy were consumed by the duke's agent and engineer. It was also said that the constable had to be sent for when the men began to sing very loudly in Mr. Brindley's room. There was even talk of an hour or two in the stocks! Whether this be true or not, the engineer, while still a bit testy, recovered his former good spirits.

When the duke was informed of the secret test, he was delighted. He slapped his thigh, took an enormous pinch of snuff, and declared happily, " 'Sblood, I'll stuff that talk of 'Duke's Folly' right down Strange's throat." An enormous sneeze followed.

He wanted to go out right then and announce the news to the world, but Mr. Gilbert advised him against it and the engineer agreed. So they settled on July 1, 1761, as the date for flooding the aqueduct.

" 'Twill be the longest ten months of my life, I confess," said his grace, reaching for his pipe and settling back in his chair with a smile of contentment that stretched from ear to ear. "After all, my name's not 'bridge water' for nothing."

And all the time there was the endless search for money. His grace, eager to keep up with the work, moved to Blaize Tavern where his engineer already resided. Many an evening we spent there going over the accounts.

"As I see it," the duke said, one night late in February, "the canal laborers are owed close to four hundred pounds."

We all nodded. The duke pulled on his pipe. "And, had it not been for John's discovery of lime, I should owe thrice that."

His engineer and agent nodded agreement. I stared stonily ahead.

"So I must raise more cash. I can't mortgage the Worsley estate, 'tis entailed, and almost everything is pledged as security on loans."

"Your grace pays interest on some seventeen thousand pounds," I added.

"That much?" breathed the duke, "soon I shall owe more than all England combined. Well, I am determined to sell some land. There is property in Whitchurch in Shropshire worth five thousand guineas. John, I want you and Icarus to sell it for me. We must have more brass and right quick, too. Men cannot eat promises."

Mr. Gilbert and I left on horseback the next morning

and in less than three days the whole business was concluded. The duke was richer by 5,548 pounds.

We stopped for the night at an inn outside Stretton, rising early the next morning in order to reach Worsley well before nightfall. We had scarcely gone a dozen miles when we came upon a gentleman in light gray frock coat and breeches walking a fine bay stallion. Riding boots of black leather turned down to reveal the tan lining. He saluted us courteously, raising his hat.

The face seemed vaguely familiar; deep inside me something stirred, but it passed in an instant. The stranger was speaking to Mr. Gilbert.

"Good day to ye. A fine winter morning, is it not?"

His face was handsome, fine dark eyes that held a straight, honest look. His complexion was darker than Mr. Gilbert's, and he was at least an inch taller.

"It is indeed, sir," replied Mr. Gilbert. "Is your horse lame?"

"Nay, nay." He looked closely at me. "May I ask your name, young sir?"

"George, sir," I replied.

"Oh." He looked disappointed.

He turned back to Mr. Gilbert and continued. "He has carried me many miles these last few days, and I must needs let him rest. 'Tis a pity though," he added, "for I have urgent business this very day. I wonder if ... but nay, 'tis impertinent of me."

"No, go on," said Mr. Gilbert.

"Well, I cannot help but note that your horse is fresh and mine, which any unbiased observer will agree is a better animal, is tired. Because my business is so pressing, I am willing to exchange my horse for yours."

Mr. Gilbert got down and examined the bay carefully. He agreed that it was fine fettle, though it had been ridden hard. Pronouncing himself satisfied, Mr. Gilbert shook hands with the stranger. They changed saddles, and the gentleman rode off at a fast trot on his new horse.

"Strange," said the agent, "I suspected a trick, but I am a shrewd judge of horses, and I had the best of that trade."

We continued our journey at the same pace. Once or twice Mr. Gilbert stopped to inspect his new horse.

"I wish I hadn't been quite so eager now, George," he said, looking carefully at each black stocking. "But I see no sign of spavins or ringbones. His wind is good too, and there is no sign of abscessing."

He remounted. "I once heard of someone trading with a highwayman whose horse was as well known as his owner. However, that gentleman had none of the look of a collector."

It was late afternoon and becoming chilly as we rode up the lane beside the Grapes. I for one was thinking of supper and a warm bed.

"Well, here we are, George," said Mr. Gilbert, turning into the stableyard at the Hall. "But wait, what's this?"

I reigned in beside him, and there, munching contentedly on a bag of oats, was the agent's roan stallion.

"There's more to this than meets the eye," he said as we stabled our animals. "I'll wager . . ."

Aubrey came hurrying out of the Mall. "Tha's to go

right in now, 'is grace is in't library."

"I fear some new disaster," said Mr. Gilbert as we hung up our cloaks and hats and hurried to the library door. Without knocking the agent entered. He stopped so suddenly that I ran into him.

Looking fearfully around his back, I expected to see piles of documents and papers falling from the table to the floor and the carpets flung back to reveal rows of figures chalked on the wood below.

Not a bit of it. His grace, dressed in his familiar brown coat, was leaning against the mantelpiece, his elbow upon it and a glass of port in his right hand. The stranger sat in the leather armchair, a churchwarden pipe in his hand. The familiar cloud of tobacco smoke wreathed the chandalier.

Both men were in earnest conversation when we burst in upon them. The stranger rose to his feet.

"Ah, the travelers return," said the duke, reaching down a clay pipe for himself and lighting a taper from the smoky fire. "I trust all went well?"

"It did your grace," replied the agent.

The duke, as if oblivious to our anxieties, took out his pipe and blew a long, thin stream of smoke from his mouth. He cleared his throat noisily. "George, I'm afraid I must release you from my employ."

"Release me, sir?" My eyes searched his face for some clue to his meaning. His companion looked equally grave. "Is my work not satisfactory?"

"But your grace," began Mr. Gilbert, "I'll vouch for George's—"

The duke waved his pipe, silencing him. "And you, John, are almost as much to blame."

"Indeed, your grace, I can't for the life of me—"

"Did ye not trade horses with this gentleman upon the road earlier today?"

"We did," I replied. "We suspected some trick, but 'twas a fair trade."

"When you become horsejobbers," said the duke, "the first rule is to learn a man's name."

The stranger had also laid down his pipe and was regarding me with the closest attention.

"For," continued the duke, a smile stealing over his face, "if you had, Icarus, you would have known . . ."

"My father," I said, "my father." And with a cry of joy, I flung myself into the outstretched arms.

"Oh, my boy, I thought I had lost thee. So many years ago. Only two days since, I waited upon John Fielding, my old friend. His news sent me post haste to Worsley."

As for me, I said nothing. I was weeping like a baby.

"Well, I suppose you will want your horse back," said Mr. Gilbert with a smile, when the excitement died down. "I knew it was too good to be true."

"Nay, sir," said my father, gazing into my face. "I would give all I had a thousand times over to find this lad."

"That may be too much, Father," I said, "around here I was worth half a man."

"Nay, tha weren't," said his grace and Mr. Gilbert in the same breath.

Postscriptum
(1774)

It is now a dozen years since the events described in these pages took place. I might not have taken up my pen to record them had it not been for the untimely death of James Brindley. Much legend has grown around his life, and since he is no longer able to set matters straight, I have sought to do so.

My father and I stood together, hats in hand, as the aqueduct at Barton was filled. It was a glorious sight and all Lancashire seemed to be there to witness it. The water rushed through the sluices and slowly the great clay trough was filled. The arches stood firm and, as we expected, not a drop of water seeped through the masonry.

The duke was in a brand new suit that was almost as fine as that of his engineer. Lord Stamford, his grace's friend, and other guests in long flowing wigs sat in a handsome barge that was pulled across the aqueduct by a team of miners and boatmen in their Sunday best. The cheers were deafening when, just as the duke's party reached the center span, a large vessel with sails rigged passed underneath. On that day, only I was happier than the three men who had made that day come to pass. And as our Gracious Majesty had his coronation that same day, we called our event "the crowning of the arches."

A few days later, my father and I left for Bristol. He intended to retire from the sea and practice medicine in that bustling seaport. He had not remarried and now he never will.

Mr. Brindley went on to become the most important engineer in England. Some four years after the triumph at Barton, he married Anne Henshall, a young woman of my age. She undertook most of his letter writing, which was a great relief to all. Before his death, Mr. Brindley was to survey and assist in the construction of ten more canals. Indeed, so famous did he become that even when he lay dying canal builders sought his advice about a leaking canal.

"Puddle it," he told them.

They assured him they had.

"More puddle," he said, "more puddle." And then he died.

Lord Strange drew his last angry breath some three years since. He had opposed his grace to the end, leading those who refused the duke permission to cross the demesne of Sir Richard Brooke at Norton Priory. When his grace convinced Parliament once again to support him, Lord Strange died in a fit of apoplexy.

Over the years I have visited Worsley. The Duke of Bridgewater grows more eccentric as the years go by. Still sporting a brown suit made for him by the miners' tailor, he follows his interests with as much eagerness as ever. He inspects everything and uses every means to raise a few pounds wherever possible. Underground his canal moves slowly northwards while side arms burrow east and west along the coal seams. Overland the canal creeps slowly towards Manchester in the east, and Liverpool in the west. As of this writing, his grace's debt is almost one quarter of a million pounds, and it is said that this indebtedness will increase for at least ten more years as his projects progress.

And at Worsley, the duke's coal emerges on the narrow boats, the works yard is a scene of ceaseless activity, and the miners dig all day long. Ashton Tongue, the duke's master miner, tells me that the underground canals will stretch almost fifty miles before all the coal under Walkden Moor is won. There is even talk of a canal below the main level.

Mr. Gilbert, his grace's agent, still prospers, though few outside Lancashire know his name. He has invested wisely, purchasing the Golden Hill estate, through which the Trent and Mersey Canal flows. His blacklead mine at Borrowdale and the factory for it at Worsley supply work for many who would else starve. He had partnerships in salt works, lime kilns, and collieries. In 1765 the duke helped him buy Clough Hall as a reward for his many labors. My father and I are welcome guests at this fine country house with its twenty bedrooms and, yes, mahogany paneling.

And Peg. What of Peg? Why I married her in Worsley some five years after the crowning of the arches. She sits by my side as I write these lines and the twins, Robert and John, sleep peacefully upstairs. We are as content and happy as any four people on earth. And so farewell.

GOD SAVE HIS ROYAL
MAJESTY